Love Finds a Way

Love Finds a Way

MARÍA T. RAMOS

ISBN: 978-0-692-93527-9

Cover montage photos from Pixabay.com.

Design, and typography:
Héctor R. Pérez
HRP Studio

Printed by CreateSpace, an Amazon.com Company.

Dedication

To the many loves in my life,
my children, my husband, my family and grandson.
Love is now, forever is another dimension.
We don't know what tomorrow will bring,
rejoice and live for what we have today.

I love you.

TABLE OF CONTENTS

Chapter One: 1   Barefoot in the Park

Chapter Two   11   Life history—3 women

Chapter Three   17   Memories of Time Passed

Chapter Four   27   I Dream of Istanbul

Chapter Five   35   Kuşadasi

Chapter Six   47   Santorini

Chapter Seven   65   Crete

Chapter Eight   71   Rhodes

Chapter Nine   73   Chios & Mykonos

Chapter Ten   77   Athens

Chapter Eleven   81   Return to Reality

Chapter Twelve   91   Aloneness

Chapter Thirteen   97   We've Only Just Begun

CHAPTER ONE

BAREFOOT IN THE PARK

*I*t's springtime in late May, early June, a wonderful time of the year. The change from the coldness of winter to spring has a profound effect. Nature awakens in the springtime, it's a time of renewal and rebirth. Colorful flowers forming bouquets in bright red, blue, pink, purple, white and yellow are blooming and showing off their beauty and fragrance. Buds start growing and leaves are reappearing on the trees. In the spring the city is vibrant and the weather is warm for this time of the year. It's a time of letting go of past events, making room for new adventures, journeys, opportunities and challenges. Life moves on to renew itself and people are celebrating the fresh air, the sun's warmth, the outdoors and welcoming the new season.

Jules has just left his office in mid-Manhattan. He and his attorney were discussing a lawsuit he filed some time ago. After two years, the case still does not have a trial date and he's grown impatient and is contemplating a voluntary dismissal of the case. His attorney advised against this and convinced him otherwise. Jules has sustained a considerable amount of losses in stock investments, attorney's fees and associated costs. The suit is against a brokerage company on investments they made through a firm which invested in fraudulent stock options. If he wins the case he will be able to recoup his losses and get millions of dollars back.

The defendants in the lawsuit had made false and misleading statements trying to increase the trading volume and share price of the company's stock by falsely naming well-known companies as customers and making highly misleading projections about investment returns. Jules was livid because he is an expert on stock options and he had confided in a broker he had worked with for years and did not realize he had invested his money in a company unknown to him. The broker argued that the investment was based on the company's promising historical charts. The broker authorized use of Jules's company name to lure other investors without Jules's knowledge and authorization. This was similar to other

Security Exchange Commission cases under investigation.

Jules leaves the building and tells his driver to leave. He just wanted to walk through Central Park to release some of the tension and frustration he is feeling about the case. The park is full of joggers, kids playing ball, skaters, musicians, parents walking with strollers, and people walking to work. As he walks through the park he sees a couple sitting on a blanket with their shoes off and it reminds him of all of the years that have passed since he last saw Suzanne. He starts thinking of all the beautiful memories they had shared together. His face lightens up and he begins to smile alone as he decides to take off his jacket and fold it on top of his briefcase on a bench in the park. He takes off his shoes and socks and he stands barefoot on the grass and remembers the days he had spent with Suzanne taking afternoon strolls in the park and her falling in the lake by the boathouse near the rowboats and Gondolas in the heart of the park. He really enjoyed her company. Such great memories. He was laughing alone, reliving moment by moment her smile, when they first met at a local strip club where she was a stripper.

Together they enjoyed the New York City Broadway shows and he reminisced about going sailing on a friend's yacht and his getting sea sick. It was as though someone was tickling him. Thinking of her left him breathless. He would close his eyes and inhale and exhale and a smile would appear and brighten his face. He had not felt so relaxed in such a long time. For the first time in a long time he didn't feel his usual anger about his empty life. People in the park would walk by and smile as though they were reading his thoughts. "He who's laughing to himself his evil deeds is recalling." It was a memory he would always cherish.

His facial expression started to change when he remembered when the relationship came to an end. He traveled back in time to the moment when Suzanne told him she could no longer keep up with him and his fast-paced life. She wanted to settle down and he was not ready. His idea of settling down was coming home to her, going out to a romantic dinner with her or with friends. She wanted to raise the family she never had. She had left home for a better life because her father was an alcoholic and there was no future for her where she lived.

All of the travel from city to city, his work in the airline industry and his other business ventures demanded time and attention from him. It became impossible for her to keep up with him, he was never home or being home he would work late. When she tried to approach him on the subject of commitment, he brushed her off and would say that they had a wonderful relationship, why spoil it. He suggested that she enroll in a local university and obtain a degree. It wasn't a farfetched idea, she had always wanted to go back to school, but felt humiliated by his suggestion. It made her feel the difference that existed in their upbringing and educational background.

The airline industry was not what he had expected. It simply didn't work, not because it wasn't successful, but, because it wasn't a challenge for him to build airplanes. It was great for about two years, while he learned the business, but he started to miss the excitement of buying and selling stock as he had done in the past.

He had gone into the aircraft manufacturing business because he wanted to run a large scale business and settle down. He did not know much about manufacturing aircraft, but he had the money needed to invest. He had investigated several companies and became very interested in a leading aircraft manufacturer who was struggling financially. He had met with the company's CEO and they had discussed company contracts, assets, inventory, employment, salary ranges, and unions before he decided to invest. The company had built modern and efficient aircraft. They had the design and production of individual components and had major airlines buying their product.

The company had fallen behind on IRS payments and were in the process of an embargo when Jules finally decided to invest and pull them out of their financial crisis.

After about a year he realized he was too involved in the company's management. He began to resent the contractual agreement he had made. The industry was growing in great proportions, they had all the contracts with the airlines. Business was booming and they were building lots of aircraft for the Air Force and the Navy and were also negotiating private contracts.

The business was exciting for a while, he loved all of the negotiations and making deals, but after a while it was more of the same. Jules's dissatisfaction and frustration grew and was written all over his face and it was felt by his colleagues and especially Suzanne. It was a drastic change for him and as much as he tried, it was impossible to digest the changes he had made thinking of a future with Suzanne.

One afternoon Suzanne called and met with Jules's associate, Bryan for lunch. She was concerned and curious to learn whether or not Jules was miserable at work. She asked Bryan for his opinion and he told her that they argued a lot at work, that it was very difficult to work with him and he himself was on the verge of leaving the company. He had received a job offer from a competitor and was considering the offer, but his colleagues would not allow it, because he knew the business better than anyone else in the industry. Suzanne told him that it was very difficult for them at home. Jules had distanced himself and he seemed cold, reserved and was shutting her out of their relationship. It was extremely painful for her and she simply wanted to understand what was going on at work with him. She had mixed feelings and did not know if he was stressed because of her or pressure at work and she did not want to complicate matters any more than they were. She apologized to Bryan for meeting with him, but was desperate because she truly loved Jules and wanted to make the relationship work between them.

Suzanne had laid her arm on the table, and Bryan put his hand on top of hers, trying to console her. It was a very innocent and friendly gesture on his part. At that precise moment Jules walked up to them and saw Bryan's hand on Suzanne's. They both pulled their hands back and looked at him surprised. Jules asked if it was a private meeting because he was not invited to lunch. Suzanne looked at him and said, "Jules, sit down and join us for lunch. I was just asking Bryan about information on the local universities and which one he recommended for me to attend."

Jules asked her, "Well, which one did he recommend," ignoring Bryan.

She responded, "We haven't discussed that yet, it was a surprise I had for you."

Jules said, "A surprise for me?," and asked if there were other surprises he didn't know about.

Suzanne ignored his comment and Bryan started to get up to leave, but Suzanne said, "Please don't leave, stay for lunch. It's already been ordered."

Jules was extremely jealous and suspicious and did not try to hide his feelings. It was not the first time Bryan and Suzanne had talked alone. He remembered the time at a company activity when he saw her talking to Bryan. Suzanne tried to fix the situation but it had already turned tense. Jules stayed for lunch and Bryan told Suzanne that of all the universities in the city, he could only recommend two that had an excellent finance curriculum.

Jules asked Suzanne why did she want to study finance, and she explained that she wanted to learn more about his line of work and about investments. Jules told Suzanne that he could teach her and she would learn from the best (sarcastically). Suzanne knew that Jules wanted her to study, so that she could have a level of education that would allow her to participate in activities with other women who were members of Women's Civic Clubs and philanthropic organizations. He knew that most of the women were professionals and he knew how conceited, arrogant and superior they could act, unlike Suzanne, who was caring, compassionate, unselfish and kind. He remembered she was crying at home one evening because one of the women said something humiliating to her and she never told him what it was.

Suzanne took up Bryan's advise and visited both universities prior to making a decision to enroll. She kept putting it off, wondering if she had the skills to attend college and pursue a degree in finance. It seemed unbelievable and out of reach for someone with her upbringing. She had attended high school as an adolescent, but never liked it and she would play hooky from school every day. She was lucky to have finished school when she did because, soon after, she left home. She gave herself an opportunity to get a high school diploma because she didn't want to continue wasting her life like her friends without any ambition or direction. In her home town education was the worse, teachers didn't care and the Board of Education would hire the worst teachers in her district. They would give passing grades just for showing up at the front door and taking an exam, which she did. Unlike her friends she would read her classmates' notes and pass her exams. Well, at least she had a high school diploma which would allow her to get a decent job once she moved out of her parents' house. It certainly was not a home. She felt awkward wanting to go back to school, not knowing how to sit and study and concentrate because she never did learn how. She didn't know anyone her age who was going to college and felt like a complete failure. She did not want to entertain the thought of her embarrassment of failure before Jules.

Suzanne would force herself to stop thinking about school and would devote her attention to the beautiful ten-room country home where she lived with Jules. It was a beautiful two-story Victorian house. There were three large family rooms with built in fireplaces and entertainment centers. The kitchen was close by and had access to the dining room, which had a rather long dinner table with twenty chairs. Suzanne could never imagine what it would be like to entertain so many people. One of the family rooms was connected to the large living room, which was larger than the three family rooms together. He and Suzanne always sat in the same corner in the living room, it was their favorite spot. Every other place seemed too impersonal.

On the second floor there were two master bedrooms, a bath with a gorgeous jacuzzi and a huge walk-in closet. The three other bedrooms had large walk-in closet space.

The home had been built by an architect for his family and when their children became older and were living in their own homes, he and his wife decided to find a small apartment for themselves. The house had a beautiful extended front porch and a barn where they kept horses which Suzanne had loved from the moment she saw them. The house was her dream home and she loved living there. Nothing in her dreams had prepared her to be so happy.

Jules knew she was crazy in love with the house and he remembered her walking into several antique stores looking for something special to hang in the porch. After a while she finally found and purchased the perfect sign which read "Home Sweet Home," and it certainly was.

Jules knew that Suzanne loved him and loved their home. She went from city girl to country girl, although she had lived and was raised in a small town. She enjoyed horseback riding with him and always made sure she was up early to have breakfast with him in the morning. After being in the house day in and day out, decorating and redecorating and organizing the same things over and over again, she realized she needed something other than playing housekeeping. She realized that she wanted to do more and become involved in local civic activities. She contacted a woman she had met at one of the many dinner parties she and Jules had attended. She asked her about local activities and clubs she could join. The woman invited her over for lunch the next day with some friends that were meeting to volunteer for several fund raising events in benefit of cancer patients at a local hospital. At the meeting they tossed around ideas such as concerts, golf tournaments, and lunch or dinner fund raisers. Suzanne was very excited in participating in every event and convinced Jules to have a dinner party to raise funds at their home. Suzanne was very active and volunteered for every activity. Her participation in the events helped her meet more people and feel as though she was part of something important. She convinced herself that it was a wonderful idea and she wanted to do more. She would visit patients at the hospital and would read books to small children. Her drive was pushing her and she was seeking fulfillment. She wanted to do more. There was no stopping her, she was determined to succeed. She wanted to feel there were no boundaries, no obstacles or challenges that she could not overcome.

Jules had truly inspired her to believe in herself. She would have lived only for his love, but Jules was not ready to commit and he insisted on the prospect of her obtaining a college degree. The more she thought about going to college, the more she felt it would interfere with their life and her volunteer work. She saw herself as fulfilling her dreams with Jules by her side and by helping others. She could no longer settle for a simple life at home after the accomplishments she had made in raising thousands of dollars for a good cause. Jules and his colleagues commented about Suzanne's way of getting funds for the cause. Jules would say, "Well you know what they say about city girls, you can take the girl out of the city but you can never take the city out of the girl." What he really meant was that in her profession as a stripper she had power! Everyone whom she spoke to, she convinced for a donation. She had a natural ability to persuade people to think the way she wanted them to think and she was in control.

Her accounting was impeccable, she kept books on all donations received and expense receipts. She kept track of the money that was donated. One of her original ideas implemented by the committee was to spend the donations on purchasing hospital equipment and products, beds, or paying for services rather than donating money. She wanted to know exactly where each cent was being spent. This idea and her not getting paid for her services was what appealed to the donors and she used this strategy to her advantage.

Suzanne did not cease to surprise Jules. He was a lucky guy, she was smart and witty and would call him every time she received a donation. After all, no one wanted word to get out that they were a cheapskate and were not cooperating with her cause.

Every night Suzanne would ask Jules for advice on handling the donations and she wanted to know what to say during the weekly meetings with the committee.

At home, as time passed, Jules grew distant. Suzanne started to devote more time to him and would talk less about her work. She started working less and spending more time at home, making sure she was home before he arrived. One evening, when he arrived, Jules seemed more indifferent and distant than usual. His coldness frightened her and she feared that she had lost him. She had tried everything imaginable to make the relationship work to the extent of sacrificing the time she dedicated to her volunteer work. She suddenly realized it was her queue to move on before the relationship worsened. She always imagined herself with Jules as a couple enjoying life, but with his behavior, she was no longer able to see him in the same picture with her. Suzanne felt he longed for the life he had before they met. She knew that he loved her, but their worlds were so apart, so different, although they lived in the same house, their upbringing and their education was different. Oftentimes in dinner gatherings when Suzanne attended, she would be silent all evening and would not participate in the conversation for fear of saying or asking something inappropriate that would embarrass the two of them. She had already learned from experience.

One evening an overly talkative wife said to her, "Honey, cat got your tongue? Why haven't you said a word all evening. Doesn't Jules let you speak in public?," and started laughing.

Suzanne was so embarrassed and she responded by saying, "Actually, I'm quite talkative, but today you've taken the lead for everyone, not even Jules has had an opportunity to say much. But, please, don't stop, I think everyone is enjoying your loud laughter, drunkenness and drivel conversation. I'm I not right Jules?"

Jules looked at her and said, "What she means is that you have made very good interpretations and we are all captivated, aren't we, dear," looking at Suzanne.

"Yes, of course," she responded.

Suzanne did not speak because she was self-conscious about the limitations in her educational background and she was apprehensive and feared being recognized by someone who knew about her past life as a stripper. It was just as difficult for her when she participated in the fund raisers always fearing someone would recognize her. It wasn't as though her past had happened a long time ago, it was fairly recent. She always tried to have a wonderful smile, but thoughts of her past kept creeping up and entertaining her mind. She wanted to keep up with Jules's expectations of her, but was very cautious. It pleased her to have him by her side. His love gave her so much satisfaction, security and peace.

Deep down inside, behind the smiles and the love she had for him, she realized she was not living up to the expectations she wanted of herself. Suzanne finally admitted that both of them were falling apart and there were circumstances in his life which made them both miserable. It had not been a well thought out decision for them to move in with each other and the pressure was continuously intensifying between them.

They both kept clinging on to each other, not wanting to accept what both of them knew was inevitable. Both realized they had to go their separate ways. He did not know how to break away. Suzanne was not one of his usual casual relationships where he would break off and move on. He was not emotionally detached from Suzanne, as he was with other women.

Jules knew his relationship with Suzanne was different, she was not like the other women in his life interested in the worldly goods he could offer. She was interested in him, not in what he could give her. His life with Suzanne was full of surprises, there was so much more involved, they enjoyed their mutual company and laughed together and they read each other's mind by simply looking at each other. She had a wonderful sense of humor which complemented a side of him that only she could bring out. She knew what Jules wanted in their intimate moments. She pleased him in every way possible; just touching him was enough for him to sit back and let Suzanne play with him. She would let him hunger for her until his desire for her lead him to desperately hold her and touch her breast and softly caress her inner legs and softly work himself upward and downward feeling her entire body and pulling her towards him until they both reached that ultimate moment at the height of the mountain top where they had joined together as one. They enjoyed the pleasure of their intimacy and would enjoy each other so much they could never get enough of each other. When he closed his eyes and thought of her he could feel himself inside of her body.

Aside from their wanting each other, loving each other and filling each other's lives with joy and laughter, his lack of commitment in what she considered a stable and solid relationship set them apart and ruined their relationship. The unasked and unanswered question between them was, how do you break away and detach yourself from the one you love without feeling that your world is crumbling, your heart is heavy and the pain is too great to endure?

Suzanne knew he had fulfilled all of her dreams, he had filled her life with so much love, abundance and security, but she wanted more. It was not out of selfishness but rather a sense of wholeness. She asked herself if she was being selfish having so much and still feeling she wanted more. The answer was easy, it was not the possessions he could give her, but what he could give of himself—his heart, his commitment, himself.

The sparkle in their eyes had diminished, not for lack of love. She wanted something he could not give her and she could not settle for what he would be willing to give. They simply could not continue to live under a false pretense of what each expected of one another without shattering each other's life. It was more difficult staying together than parting.

At home, the pressure was felt intensely, they were good for each other, but they were making believe there was nothing wrong and their relationship became unbearable. Suzanne sensed his uneasiness and distance, although Jules was making an effort to continue the relationship, but even in intimacy it had become strained.

Suzanne finally decided to leave. She had her suitcase at the door when he arrived home. It was her intention to leave without saying a painful goodbye, but he arrived early that day. He had felt a crushing pain in his chest, as though his heart knew she would leave and there was nothing to save them and keep them together. In absolute silence they simply looked at each other and smiled away their goodbyes. He kissed her forehead, closed his eyes, held her hand and as she walked away still holding one hand, their fingers touching, they finally let go and she closed the door behind her.

As she walked away, Jules started to open the door, but hesitated. Suzanne turned her head excited when she heard the doorknob click, thinking he would open the door and ask her not to leave, but he didn't, and she left in tears.

He did not realize how much he loved her until after she left and days passed by without her. He just sat quietly on the sofa with a drink in hand, teary eyed and starring into the glass as though there would be something magical in his reflection which would bring her back. When she left his heart sank. He finally realized he was going to lose her. He realized he loved her like no other woman, she had robbed his heart. But, he kept hesitating and knew that he was not ready to give Suzanne what she wanted and convinced himself that it was a good decision.

The days that followed were difficult for him. He missed her so much it was as though all of the air had disappeared and he was asphyxiating and gasping for air. He realized she was his lifeline and he could not breathe without her. He was so devastated. He had not realized how much he depended on Suzanne's relationship. Her presence made him feel alive.

As days went by, they turned into weeks and months and years. He still remembered her and knew it was his fault the relationship did not continue because he would not commit and take the relationship to another level.

CHAPTER TWO

STORIES OF LIFE HISTORY—THREE WOMEN

*S*uzanne had a very poor upbringing and poor manners. She was a tomboy as a child and as she grew up she made terrible selections with respect to men. Her mom and dad did not have a good education. He was a car mechanic who learned the trade from his daddy. Her mother learned to sew and made some money sewing. She was very good at it and would make her own patterns and clothing. She also received government help, for herself and her children. Their home environment was peaceful when their dad wasn't home, because he was drunk all the time. They never reported his income or that he lived with them. He was an alcoholic and would drink away his weekly pay check. Suzanne and her mom would end up supporting him. He was never able to support his family.

The schools in the area did not offer a good education to the students. It seemed they wanted to keep kids ignorant and not smart enough to go to college. People in general did not have any goals in life except to get married and have kids. There was no one to look up to as a mentor, no aspirations other than working at a local business in town. Suzanne did not like being a seamstress like her mom; she preferred to work as a waitress and bartender at one of the local bars.

She soon learned that if she wanted to grow up and do something, she definitely had to head out of town. She finally made the big decision and left home to find a better life and a good education. She had no job experience, except for working at the bar.

She ended up in Los Angeles, which looked so glamorous in the movies and magazines. When she arrived she found a cheap apartment and a temporary job at a bar. This is where she met Layla and Andrea and they immediately became friends and roommates.

They all had a similar upbringing. Andrea escaped from a house you could hardly call home. Her mom was a nurse who worked long hours to avoid her abusive alcoholic husband. Andrea was the oldest and would care for her younger siblings until her dad hit her and she ran away from home to her aunt's house.

Her aunt was a doctor and would talk to her about her work at the hospital and encouraged Andrea to study medicine. Her dreams of ever becoming a doctor were shattered when her aunt's husband fell in love with her. It became increasingly difficult to live in the house with them because he would constantly bother her when her aunt was not home. She then went back home to help her mom because her dad had fallen ill and there was no one to care for her siblings and her dad while her mom was working.

Andrea then enrolled in school to get her high school diploma and was able to enroll at the local university. She and her mom had managed to work different schedules to be able to care for the children. Her mother was very appreciative of her efforts and helped her to have enough time for her studies, and as a result Andrea got a scholarship and went to another university with a pre-med program. Her mother helped her as much as she could, but housing expenses were more than her mother could afford and Andrea had to start waitressing. The tips were good, her work schedule was flexible and it did not conflict with her school schedule. She was able to pay her rent and expenses and send her mom a check almost every week to help with her family.

When she started working, she met Layla and later Suzanne. They became friends and soon found an apartment the three could share, and they became family.

Layla's mom was very loving, she had three kids from different dads and all the dads provided child support. Occasionally, a new "uncle" would visit them and leave some money. Layla grew up thinking it was good to have so many uncles until she was old enough to understand they were mom's customers.

Layla's mother was beautiful and she finally met a man that wanted to marry her and be a father to Layla and her siblings. It was not easy for Layla to have someone permanently living in the house and giving her orders as though he was her real dad. He was very strict and she had to cook and clean more than usual while her mother sat around all day long acting as though she was a queen and her children were her subjects.

Layla felt she was Cinderella—fitting the part where she was in rags, but not necessarily becoming a rich princess. She grew very tired of being ordered around and babysitting and cleaning and cooking. One day she left home and promised to never return. She then hopped on a bus, left town and went as far as she could with the money she had for a bus ride to wherever. The destination was of little concern, she just wanted to leave and be free. She had taken the first bus ride available and did not know if it would take her to San Francisco, Fargo, Oakland or to Los

Angeles. When she got off the bus at the last stop she found herself in Los Angeles. She had cried herself to sleep during her journey.

It was difficult leaving home, because even though she was tired and was desperate to leave, she had left behind her mom, whom she loved dearly, and her siblings. It was difficult for her to think how life would be without them, and how their lives would be without her. They were so used to having her around and they would all cuddle up to sleep with her at night. She knew that they would miss her terribly, but she was just too tired and fed up of being the big sister and of her mother's not assuming her responsibility as a parent and relying on her.

Once in Los Angeles she had to rent a very inexpensive room and find a job quickly to support herself. After searching endlessly, she was able to land a job in a striptease club. There were no other jobs available, but luckily this is where she met Andrea and later Suzanne.

The three became friends instantly, they all had similar stories. They had all left their troubled homes in small towns to find a better future for themselves and they all had a good loving mother that had cared for them and they missed terribly.

The three of them became very attached to each other. There was a sisterly bond between them. Layla would like to sleep around a lot like she had learned from her mom. She had many male friends that would provide for her. Suzanne and Andrea would argue with her, but she would not allow them to interfere in her personal life, until she dated a man that beat her up so severely that she was in the hospital for days. This finally made her decide that she did not want to have any more relationships with men. She was done!

Layla decided to go back to school after Andrea convinced her about a nursing career. Andrea took her to the hospital on a tour to meet some of her patients and the hospital staff. After spending time with Andrea and seeing all of the patients who were sick in the hospital, she felt guilty about complaining about her life. Her problems seemed so small compared to the pain she saw in the eyes of patients with incurable diseases. There were adults of all ages, children, and the medication would not always ease their pain.

She decided that this was the career she wanted to pursue, for the first time in her life she felt she could help people and not feel like at home where she was ordered to do things.

She wanted to dedicate her life to being of service to others. She felt renewed and alive, better than she had ever felt even as a little girl. For once in her life she could make decisions without anyone dictating to her what she had to do. Andrea had helped her find herself and she set meaningful goals for her future. Layla had a new direction in life, she was no longer guided by the life she had known and learned from her mother. She realized she could live independently and not depend on anyone for her survival. She was a decision maker, independent and self-supporting. Layla had a new north and was eager to commence her new life, it was as though she had been hypnotized and had lived an illusion all her life based on a misguided upbringing by her mom. Layla knew that her mother was influenced by her mom and she simply did not have the courage to leave town as she had done.

During this time she had met Suzanne, who was new in town. She must have also taken a bus to any town and found herself looking for a place to sleep and work. She too found a job in a bar that was hiring dancers and waitresses. She started waitressing and realized how much more money she could earn as a stripper. Suzanne hated being a stripper and have men ogling at her, although she had to admit she did have a great body, tall, thin and very long beautiful legs. The tips were very good and soon she would be able to get a nice apartment with Layla and Andrea. Layla shared her secret of finding eligible married men willing to spend their money with healthy women rather than sleeping around. Layla had told her to find men that could be regulars. This would eventually result in not having to continue stripping in bars or waitressing. Suzanne did not like the idea and didn't know if it was worse to sleep around or to be a stripper. This was not what she expected when she left home. She was seriously contemplating going back home with her family. She was between a rock and a hard place.

She decided to continue job hunting and try to find a job which did not require sleeping or stripping. Most of the jobs she found were as a maid, cashier or in a fast food chain. She would have had to work three shifts, find three jobs, work 12-hour days and weekends in order to make ends meet.

Suzanne was an attractive woman, not polished or chic, but she had a way of smiling with her eyes and it would brighten up anyone's day. She was quiet—not talkative—which was appealing. She then met several men which seemed nice enough to become regular customers. She maintained a regular relationship with three of them and with their support and her job waitressing, and occasionally stripping when one of her coworkers didn't show up for work or called in sick, she could pay for her apartment and expenses and save to go to college.

Suzanne wanted to study, but was unsure which courses she should study; she was still young and did not really want to be a full-time student. She just lived day to day, not knowing what direction to take. Her upbringing did not provide her the stability she needed to make decisions about the present or the future. Trying to figure out what to study was a difficult task for her.

Suzanne was not looking to meet someone who would provide for her and make a commitment and marry her and live happily ever after. She knew that was for dreamers, and although she liked to day dream, she always saw herself as a working woman in a large corporation making big decisions. Suzanne did not think about someone to make her happy; if by chance she met someone it would be to complement each other.

Her instability, lack of confidence in herself and her insecurity did not provide her with the necessary tools she needed to make sound decisions and allow her to become an independent, self-starter, motivated woman.

Her continued dependence to be supported by others just kept her going around in circles with no outlet to give her an opportunity for a better life. She was in a rut and Layla and Andrea could not convince her otherwise.

CHAPTER THREE

MEMORIES OF TIME PASSED

A small boy kicks over a red, white, yellow and blue beach ball to him and he awakens from his day dream with the past. It appears as though Suzanne's departure was recent, but time had passed and she had left a long, long time ago. As he remains seated, there's a Chicago song playing at a distance:

> Saturday in the Park
> I think it was the Fourth of July
> People dancing, people laughing
> A man selling ice cream
> Singing Italian songs
> 'Eh cumpari, ci vo sunari'...

He smiled as he stood up and started walking towards the sidewalk to catch a cab. As he's leaving the park he sees a fancy café named "Rush Hour" at a short distance. The name of the café called his attention because he was always rushed. The restaurant was in the middle of the street in between two tall buildings and he decided to walk in. It's mid-morning and as he walks in he picks up the morning newspaper from the counter and the waitress escorts him to a small table with two chairs by the window, away from the morning sun.

The café looked rather small from the outside, but surprisingly, it was big inside with about 20 tables with tiffany stained glass ceiling lamps decorated with colorful designs of grapes, apples, pears and fruits. The lamps looked very stylish and colorful, and they were hanging over the tables with dimmed lights. The tables were covered with red and white checkered tablecloths and the chairs were dark cheery wood with red leather cushion seats.

A young woman about 25 years old walks over to him to take his order. He looks at her briefly and orders coffee and bagels. When she arrives and serves his order, she stares at him, but he continues sipping his coffee and reading the newspaper, not perceiving her stare. The restaurant was not very crowded and it was nice, quiet and relaxing compared to the bustling and crowded city streets. It was so quiet that you could not hear any of the noise in the streets. Occasionally outside noise would creep in when someone came into the café or left. It was as though the windows and walls were soundproof.

As he read the newspaper and drank his coffee, he hears what seems to be very familiar voices. There were two women about his age speaking in French and they were accompanied by two younger girls. The women were sitting across the table from him. The first one was in her fifties. She was dressed in black slacks and beige sandals. Her blond hair was loose and uncombed. It seemed like she had gotten out of bed late and ran to the café to meet up with her friends. The other one was very nicely dressed. She was very thin, wearing a beautiful cream colored dress with high heels. She had short black hair and had a huge diamond ring on her finger and a very expensive wrist watch. The two young girls called her "mom." They were about 20 years old and looked like twins. They were dressed in jeans with fashionable blouses and bags, and the waitress that had taken his order was sitting at the table with them. They were having breakfast and they laughed and spoke as though they were very good friends or family.

The woman's voice seemed so familiar, but he simply could not remember where he had met her. As he continued reading the newspaper she suddenly laughed out loud and said something in French and he looked up to see her. He suddenly remembered where he had met her, he could not believe it was her, but he couldn't remember her name. She was much older now and he immediately had a flashback of the time he had met her. She was Suzanne's friend. He thought it was impossible, this woman was very different, very sophisticated and chic. It could not possibly be her.

She continued to speak in English and tried to control her loud and distinct laughter. It took him a few minutes to react, but there was no mistake. It was Layla, he finally remembered her name. He could not resist the temptation and walked across the table to where they were seated and asked, "Excuse me, this may sound like a familiar line, but, have we met before?, do we know each other?, you look so familiar."

When they looked up and saw him, their eyes opened wide, they recognized him immediately. It was Jules. They both looked surprised and the woman with blond hair smiled and was about to say something to him, but the other woman put her hand on her friend's hand and made believe she didn't know him and told him in French that he had mistaken them for someone else.

He apologized and was both puzzled and unsure if it in fact was her after what had just transpired when she put her hand over her friend's hand. As he walked back to his table, the waitress followed him and asked if he'd like to order anything else and offered him more coffee. As he raised his eyes to look at her, they both looked into each other's eyes. There was a certain familiarity in their eyes. He was contemplating how beautiful she was, tall, thin and beautiful. Her eyes were deep and penetrating, as were his. She looked as though she was about to reveal a secret and opened her mouth to say a word, but suddenly hesitated. She stared at him and after a few minutes of looking at every detail in his face, she apologized and said, "Now I'm the one thinking that we have met before."

She kept staring at him in disbelief and smiled. It wasn't uncomfortable for either of them, because there was something so special about her and she looked like someone he knew. What he did not know was that she knew who he was. There was a bond between them that reached and touched their hearts profoundly.

She thought to herself, "I am finally meeting him after so many years." She always read all the articles published in the newspapers and she said, "I apologize again for staring, aren't you Jules Quinn? I have read all the newspaper articles about your success in the industry and I can't believe that you are here."

He responded that he was Jules Quinn and smiled and asked if they had met before because she seemed so familiar to him. She did not respond. He could not take his eyes off her as she walked away. It was a very unsettling and unusual feeling, something he had not experienced with any woman before.

As he was waiting for her to bring him the bill, he saw the French woman walk outside of the restaurant and a car drove up, picked up the two girls she was with and drove off.

As he was about to stand and walk to the counter the woman had walked back to the restaurant, sat next to him and her friend followed and sat on his left side. They both said a synchronized "Hello Jules."

And Andrea continued, "Of course we've met before. We are Suzanne's friends, Layla and Andrea. I didn't realize it was you until you walked over to our table."

Layla said, "I recognized you immediately and didn't want you to say anything in front of my girls."

Jules just sat there between the two women, shaking his head and not knowing what to say. He finally looked at Layla and said, "You have changed, but you could not have ever changed your laughter." Jules then recalled Andrea.

They immediately started a conversation, but Andrea had to leave to go to the hospital where she worked as a doctor. Layla stayed behind to talk with Jules. She wanted to know what he had done for the past

25 years or so since they had last seen each other. She started telling him about the fairy tale story she had lived and all the wonderful things that had happened to her.

Her life had changed, it took a twist for the better. She had met her husband in Los Angeles while taking a nursing course in the university.

At the time, she had been living with Suzanne and Andrea. They had been working in a strip club and she and Andrea stopped working in the club, soon after Suzanne left. Andrea had been waitressing in other clubs because of the tips in order to continue her med school career while she completed her studies.

She had met her husband in the university, who was studying for a semester under a student exchange program from a university in France. He wanted to visit the U.S. and was taking several accounting and finance courses with Suzanne. She had introduced them one day in the cafeteria while they were in between classes.

"He sat next to me and asked if I lived in LA. He was looking for someone to take him sightseeing. I answered that I was not a tourist guide, that there were tourist guides in the local travel agencies. He responded that he did not want to feel like a tourist, he just wanted to tour the city and sites as a Californian."

She could not resist laughing and told him she was too busy with her work and studies and she did not have the extra time for touring. He kept insisting and told her he could pay her. She quickly responded that he should ask any of the beautiful girls on campus if he was just looking for a female companion. He responded that he already had all the female company that he needed.

"I asked him, why would such a handsome guy like yourself want someone like me to take you around? He responded that I was the only one who looked like a serious, no nonsense person, who would 'indeed' not like someone like him."

She laughed and agreed and responded that he was definitely not her type. "Of course—he responded—I was right in thinking you would say no and that you would not like someone like me. You see, I have already had my share of women who were interested in 'site-seeing' my dorm and you certainly don't seem the type."

She started laughing and accepted his offer to go sightseeing and said he didn't have to pay her. He only had to pay for transportation, the entrance fees and lunch or dinner if they spent all day sightseeing.

They scheduled to meet and she took him to all the touristy places in Los Angeles. They spent about two weeks together during the afternoons when they didn't have classes and she wasn't working. She was enjoying the sightseeing and enjoyed his company more than she had anticipated. He was very charming and funny and made her laugh as no one had done for a long time. One day he invited her to an amusement park. She was not thrilled with the idea but accepted to go. While on the rides in the park, they were very close to each other in the lines and even while riding on the wooden trunks and the rides. She would sit in front of him or beside him and he started to put his arms around her like the rest of the couples, or he would hold her tightly when she sat in front of him. She was not prepared for romance or a relationship, she was through with men, but he was making her feel like a schoolgirl and it made her nervous.

Her face flushed as though she was on a first date. He then played with her hair and sank his face into her hair, while on the rides. This was totally unexpected and she was not prepared to have a romance with him. When they got off the ride, she told him "NO, keep your distance, we are not dating." He respected her wishes, but was not going to give up trying. He really liked her because she was not all over him like the rest of the women.

One evening, he invited her over to his apartment for dinner. She knew very well what would come next, but accepted, after all she did like him just a little bit; well, maybe just a little bit more than just a little bit. Layla went home to change and put on a short black, sleeveless dress with a lace collar and black high heels. She knew she looked stunning.

When she arrived at the apartment, which was not a dorm as he had said, she knocked on the door and as he opened the door, they were surprised to see each other. He had not expected such a beautiful woman that was totally different from the woman he had been sightseeing with dressed in jeans, a t-shirt, sneakers and baseball cap. For the first time, he realized she had shoulder length black hair and her skin was like a porcelain doll with thick black eyebrows, big brown eyes and her pink lipstick brightened her face.

He wore black pants and a white shirt which looked very, very expensive. When they looked at each other it was as though they had never met before and were on a blind date.

They just looked at each other and remained standing at the door, until she said, "Can I come in," and he responded, "Of course, excuse my manners. I hadn't realized that you are so beautiful."

While in the apartment he had prepared dinner, or so he said. He played very soft music and served her a glass of wine. They sat down for dinner and chatted all evening about their classes. After dinner, she said it was late and had to leave to get up early the next morning to go to work. He stood in front of the door and asked her not to leave, but she insisted. He asked her to stay with him that night and he would pay her. Before he finished his sentence, she slapped him across his face. He was startled by her reaction, no one had ever slapped him before. She then told him he was a monster just like all the other men before him. She had liked him and now he had ruined the friendship by treating her in a way she had not expected from him. She demanded that he tell her how he found out about her past life as a stripper and, and… she could not bring herself to say another word. When he realized what she had done for a living, he told her that what he was about to say, before she so rudely interrupted him, was that he would make up for her day's salary, if she didn't make it to work. He said, "I just wanted to be with you, I was not paying for sex. I don't have to pay for what I can get for free," and he opened the door, rubbing his cheek where she had slapped him and said, "Please leave." He wanted to say more, but something held him back. As she stepped out of the apartment, she realized she had made a terrible mistake, but it was too late to retract herself and she left crying.

He was hopelessly in love with her. Every night he drank and slept with different women to get her off his mind. Layla was angry because she had revealed her secret and had slapped him hard. He was such a wonderful and caring man. She cried herself to sleep every night, he was like no other guy she had ever met before. They didn't see each other again after that night for a long time. As time passed by, she convinced herself that he deserved better.

She thought about what she should have done and said, but it was too late. It would have been easier to stop seeing him and tell him he was just a friend and that he had misunderstood her intentions, but it was too late—she had told him the truth.

After a few weeks, she found out that he had left and went back home to France. She did not know anything about him for months.

She would have preferred for him to think that she wasn't interested, than to destroy what he thought of her. It was difficult for her to give an explanation. She had already said the truth about her past, it was over, but she couldn't help thinking about him all day long. The two weeks she had spent with him changed her life.

One day, as she was walking in the school campus, he reappeared out of nowhere and approached her. She was both surprised and happy to see him. She had not heard anything about him for a long time. When he saw her, he told her they had to talk and invited her to dinner that evening. She was still embarrassed by her confession and behavior when they last saw each other. She had even practiced what she would say to him, if they ever saw each other again. But he caught her by surprise and she was speechless. She accepted the invitation and they agreed on a restaurant both of them knew.

When she arrived at the restaurant she didn't know what to do when she saw him with an older couple that she presumed were his parents. Layla was not prepared for this family reunion.

She turned to leave, but he had already seen her at a distance and he ran up to her. He grabbed her arm to stop her and said, "Layla, I know the truth, and you told me. It doesn't matter, I already know about you and your life. I love you, that's why I returned to find you. I thought that by leaving I would completely forget you and would never think about you again, but I was wrong. I couldn't stop thinking about you no matter how much I tried. Please don't go. Marry me Layla, we will live in France and you can have the life you deserve. You are sweet and kind and beautiful and of all the women I have ever known or dated, you are the one for me."

She looked at him and turned to leave, she did not want anything to do with him. He stopped her again and said, "Tell me you don't feel the same. Tell me that I am being stupid and foolish. Why would you deny yourself true love and happiness? It doesn't make any sense, love me, love me Layla, you are just punishing yourself. Give us an opportunity!"

Layla turned around and said, "I don't deserve this, I don't deserve you, please try to understand."

He wrapped his arms around her and said, "I am the one that doesn't deserve you. You have taught me how to be humble, loving and caring. You have changed me, ask my family. I was a playboy, irresponsible, spending my family's fortune on drugs and women, they were tired of me and sent me here with very little funds and no return ticket. They said that I could not return until I turned into a man. Layla, you did this, you are responsible for the change in me and I don't ever want to let you go. I will stay here until you accept me."

Layla melted with his words and told him she would accept him only if they gave themselves an opportunity to know each other better. After several months of spending time with each other without any intimacy between them, which was her second condition, she finally said, "Yes, I accept."

"From that day forward we have been inseparable, we married in France and have twin daughters, those which left earlier from the restaurant."

Layla had not stopped talking for about two hours, it was non-stop conversation, on and on and on. She would start a new sentence without finishing the first. All she talked about was the past twenty-five years. It was difficult for him to get a word in. He finally told her that she was very lucky to find her husband and have been married with children.

He finally asked the question that was lingering in his mind about Suzanne. He finally asked if she knew anything about her. She responded that she was fine and they had always remained in contact, even after marrying and living in France.

Layla said it was difficult for Suzanne to talk about what had happened between them when they both went their separate ways. "She was sure you would ask her to come back, but you didn't. After the breakup, she was devastated, depressed and deeply suffered your separation."

She said Suzanne had called him many times and never received a call back and after a while she stopped trying, fearing that he would reject her and the pain would be more difficult to endure.

"After about seven months of feeling sorry for herself, she finally decided to give up and forget you. She started working and studying long hours; her days were 12 and 14 hours long. She was determined to do something with her life. She went on to the university, where she obtained a degree in Business Administration with difficulty and continued to study and obtain a Master's Degree. After graduation Andrea moved on her own, I moved to France with Al, and Suzanne opened a small accounting firm with a fellow college student she had dated and they soon married."

Her marriage had not turned out well. Unfortunately, her husband ran off with her assistant and with the few funds she had left in the bank. He later died and he left her in his will. Suzanne did not know he was very rich. After he passed his father contacted her and told her about the will. She then learned that after his mom died, he left home angry and refused to speak to his father, blaming him for not being there when his mom passed. He had obtained his degree and did not rely on his family's fortune nor did he ever mention anything about his parents. When Suzanne received his inheritance, she invested part of the money in her business.

Jules was happy to finally hear about Suzanne and he asked Layla so many questions about where she lived, where her business was, and had she remarried. Layla did not want to respond to any of his questions and said to him, "Why don't you ask her daughter Laura."

Jules was so surprised to learn that Suzanne had a daughter. Layla said, "She is the waitress that took your order."

He was silent, then said, "Suzanne has a daughter!"

He was so surprised and for a few minutes was confused and realized that the reason he had stared at the waitress was because she was Suzanne's daughter and she reminded him of her. "She has a daughter!"

Layla introduced them and Laura said, "I lied when I said I had read about you in the newspapers, it was my mom who spoke to me about you all the time. She said you were very good friends and she had many fond memories of you."

He was so surprised and curious to learn all that he could about Laura, who was now sitting with both Layla and him. He started to ask her questions about her mom, wanted to know where she lived and where she was. He was surprised to learn that Laura had studied at his university and had graduated at the top of her class, just like him. She told him that she and her mom had lived in an apartment until she recently married someone she had met in college and her husband was the owner of the restaurant. She had come in to help him that morning because one of the waitresses had called in sick and her husband had an important meeting that morning.

Jules was curious to know why the restaurant was called "Rush Hour," and she said, "Mom was the one who named the restaurant after a friend that was always rushed and in a hurry."

Jules shook his head and laughed out loud, he knew he was that friend, but more important it was that she was still thinking about him. It pleased him so much.

He told Laura that he had just left his attorney's office and he thought about Suzanne as he was walking through the park. He then saw the restaurant, crossed the street without hesitating and it seemed more than just mere coincidence that he had recognized Andrea and Layla and then met her.

When he heard that Suzanne was well and he had an opportunity to see her again, his anxiety grew. He began to feel excited about seeing her. He felt as though his love for her had never left. How could he still be in love with her? It was as though they had last seen each other just hours earlier. The clock had stopped ticking for them and the universe had confabulated for them to meet again. It was as though time had stood still for them and here he was thinking about his long-lost love.

He closed his eyes and breathed deeply. Something happened, it was an irresistible feeling that attracted and pulled and pushed him towards finding her. He then asked where she was and Laura responded that she was on a flight to Athens on her way to board a cruise ship in the greek islands for eight days. He felt a force so strong that it dictated to him that he had to get on that cruise ship with her.

Jules suddenly ended the conversation and said he was late for a meeting. Laura and Layla were both perplexed at his sudden urgency to leave. He said he would return to town in about three weeks to see Suzanne and he left. He rushed out of the restaurant, pulled over a taxi and went straight to the airport. He had decided he wanted to meet up with Suzanne in Greece.

By the time he arrived at the airport his secretary had made the plane reservations for him to travel from New York's JFK airport to Athens, Greece. The cruise ship arrangements were still in the process of confirmation because his secretary had to locate a cruise ship leaving from Athens the next day for eight days in Greece. When he arrived at the airport, his driver was waiting for him with his passport and his itinerary.

Before boarding the aircraft he called a friend who worked on cruise ship bookings and asked him to book his room reservations next to hers.

His friend made the arrangements, but could not find her under the last name he had given him and he made the reservations next to the room of the only person named Suzanne that was listed as single. The agency changed the reservations and upgraded the couple that was booked next to Suzanne's room in order to accommodate Jules request. The couple were very happy, they were on their honeymoon and were given a honeymoon suite, which was much more expensive than what they had paid for. When the couple asked about the upgrade and the charges, they were told it was a raffle they had won among the cruise ship's guests.

After speaking to both his secretary and his friend Mark, the travel agent, he then boarded the plane and was finally on his way to Athens, Greece. He had never been to Greece before, this was a first for him. He was anxious to see Suzanne and wondered if she had changed or looked the same, if she had grey hair like his and whether she was still thin or fat. He started laughing to himself and pretended that she was that same beautiful woman he had met many years ago.

DAY 2 – I DREAM OF ISTANBUL

*J*ules's flight was delayed departing from New York and when he arrived in Athens, he had missed the departure of the cruise ship by an hour. He returned to the airport and had his secretary book another flight to meet the eight-day *Greek Islands Cruise* in its second docking point in Istanbul. On his way to the airport he started hesitating and kept wondering if he should go or not. He began to have doubts about his sudden decision and thought that maybe his arriving late was a sign that he should not pursue Suzanne. He called his secretary and said, "I'm going back home, book the next flight to New York and cancel my reservations to Istanbul and the cruise ship."

After a brief pause, she responded firmly, "Mr. Quinn, I'm sorry, I'm not cancelling your reservations! It took me several phone calls to book and plead for the reservations on the cruise ship, you had me upgrade a couple to be next to…— hesitating—well you know who. I know who she is now. Just go. In all of my years of working with you, you're still in love with her, that's why you have never been serious about anyone in your relationships. I'm not cancelling your reservations! If you want changes do them yourself. If it doesn't work out well, at least you tried and you won't live to regret it, you can always come back home. Give yourself the opportunity."

Jules was extremely surprised that his secretary had spoken to him in that manner. After so many years of working together, this was the first time she had ever disobeyed his requests and he answered, "You're right! I was just calling to tell you not to cancel," and he laughed. "I'm already boarding the flight to Istanbul. I really needed that, thank you."

When he arrived in Istanbul it was very late and he stayed overnight at a hotel near the dock, until the cruise ship's arrival next day near noontime. Early in the morning he hired a tour guide to take him to the different historical sites.

That day he boarded the cruise ship shortly after noon and was anxious to get ready for his dinner and finally be able to see Suzanne.

When he arrived at the cruise ship he checked in to his stateroom and was extremely nervous and tried unsuccessfully to maintain his composure. He did not like to make hasty decisions and it finally dawned on him what he had done. He had not even asked if she was with someone on the cruise, other than friends.

He then went shopping at the stores in the cruise ship and purchased some clothes, since he hadn't packed any. Everywhere he walked he would look for her and thought she must have taken a land tour before he arrived. When he looked at his itinerary, he realized he had a land tour scheduled during the day and, unfortunately, he had missed their first date together.

Once the ship took off, he became sea sick. He had purchased boxes of patches and put on two patches on his neck to avoid getting worse.

He finally felt better and started to get dressed. He changed his shirt and his suit several times, not knowing which suit to wear. He felt like a seventeen-year old going to his first high school prom. It was a mix of excitement and fear of the unknown. He finally decided to wear the black tux, it had always been Suzanne's favorite. She always said he looked so handsome when he wore a tux.

He arrived late to dinner because he kept stalling and changing shirts and ties. As he walked to the dinner table, he saw her from a distance. She was now a blonde. There she was, sitting with a beautiful red sequenced gown with a low cut back. Her back was towards him. She looked remarkably beautiful and sexy from the back. He had not seen her in so many years, he could not imagine how she looked now or if she had changed.

She had a slit in her dress which uncovered her great long beautiful leg. He inhaled deeply, closed his eyes as he got closer, and remembered the beautiful black dress she wore when he first took her to dinner. As he slowly approached the dinner table, the distance between them was less and less. He paused for a few seconds and panicked not knowing what to say when he approached her. He began getting sea sick and the room seemed to be going around in circles. He then said to himself, "Act as though it's a business meeting and you simply greet everyone at the table and act surprised to see her. Such a coincidence!"

He was so close, he could almost reach and touch her shoulder with his hand. As he started getting closer and lifted his hand to touch her, she leaned forward to talk to the man she was sitting next to. His eyes widened, he was flushed when he saw how this young man smiled and put his hand on her hand. That which he feared the most was upon him, *she was with someone.*

All he could think of was turning around and leaving as fast as he could without being noticed. His dreams of meeting with her and his expectations were shattered. What was he expecting, how could he not have asked if she was with someone. He felt so foolish and started to gasp for air, and put his hand on his heart to hold it in place.

As he turned to leave, ready to take the first step towards the exit, there she stood, in front of him. He turned to look at the woman he had almost touched, she had turned around and he saw her face and realized she was not Suzanne. As he turned towards Suzanne, he sighed in relief and whispered, "Suzanne." She was as beautiful as ever, thin, her hair was loose. She was dressed in a long black sequenced dress. Suzanne looked at him in disbelief and she stuttered as she said his name: "Juu...julllesss?"

They looked at each other and when their eyes met it seemed as though they were alone in the room, no one else existed. There was complete silence. She stopped breathing and her heart was pounding. Her heart betrayed her and she was immediately filled with the love she thought she had forgotten so long ago. When she realized what was happening, she became cautious and defensive fearing that everyone in the room could read her mind and her emotions and listen to her heart pounding. She quickly looked around the room to see who was watching her. Many questions immediately rushed to her mind: Why was he here, who was he with? She did not know if it was pure coincidence, or if he was with someone. She again said, "Jules!," in disbelief. He looked at her and tried to act as though he was there by some mere coincidence.

He responded, "Suzanne?"

There she was, the love of his life, just as beautiful as ever. How could he have ever let her go? He imagined he had turned the doorknob and opened the door back then and she rushed into his arms saying, "I love you."

Suzanne could not believe he was standing in front of her and was extremely surprised to see him. She said, "Jules, what are you doing here? I would have never thought that we would run into each other so many miles away from home and on a cruise in the Greek isles."

He acted surprised, but the real surprise was when he saw her and realized how much he was still in love with her.

Although Jules had traveled so far so see her, he had not anticipated the intensity of his love for her. He tried to compose himself. He breathed deeply, looked at her and sat down at the first chair he found. She stood next to him and asked him if he was all right and he just whispered her name, "Suzanne." It took him a few minutes to realize what had just happened.

The woman sitting with her back towards Jules turned around to welcome Suzanne to the table and told her, "Well, honey, are you just going to stand there, you're already an hour late for dinner and I'm hungry."

Suzanne could still not believe her eyes; she tried to calm herself, but it was obvious that she was very nervous and surprised. Her eyes were blinking and she just stood there confused not knowing if she should sit or stand. Jules was just as nervous, but pulled a chair so that she would sit down next to him.

The woman was one of Suzanne's friends. She was the sexiest 88 year old woman and was accompanied by a young guy 30 years old. He could have well been her great grandson. She was carrying on as though she was in her 20s, and was acting as though she had been drinking.

The waiter served the appetizers and Jules asked for a bottle of wine. They had both calmed their nerves and Suzanne repeated that she was very surprised to see him and would have never expected to meet with him there. He responded that it was a very unexpected trip, but he was extremely happy to see her and see how beautiful she still was.

Afterwards, while eating dinner, Mae asked Suzanne, "Where did you find the hunk?," as she turned her face towards Jules direction and raised her chin showing Suzanne whom she was referring to. She then continued, "Well you finally took my advice. Is he full time or part time; maybe we can share?"

Suzanne's faced flushed, she was so embarrassed, but Jules smiled and responded by saying he was full time, and he and Suzanne laughed. It was the perfect comment for him and Suzanne to relax. Mae continued the conversation by saying, "What a shame," and she winked at Jules.

She then told Suzanne she had forgotten her manners and should introduce her to lover boy. Suzanne was visibly upset with her friend, but Jules introduced himself and she said her name was Mae, but that he could call her Bae or honey. Mae then asked if he was the same Jules she had read about in the papers. He responded that there were many with his name and smiled and she said, "There is only one that Suzanne dated."

It was an awkward conversation and Mae's escort interrupted and said it was a pleasure to have him join their dinner table.

They had their first dinner and spent time together. During dinner they were silent, with an occasional nod and smile. That evening everyone introduced themselves to Jules, they had already done so the night before.

At the dinner table there was a young woman, Rachel with her parents, she could not keep her eyes off David, Mae's escort. She tried to sit as close as she could to David when she wasn't with her parents. They would follow her every move. Her parents were an older couple, they were very strict with their daughter and she had to dress very conservatively. She was very beautiful, always wearing very old fashioned clothing with long dresses, long sleeves and blouses buttoned to her neck, not at all suitable for a cruise ship. Her parents would not let her out of their sight.

The others at the table were a woman with her two teenage girls. They were about 16 years old and were connected to their music and earphones all day long. The mother had recently widowed and she took the girls on the cruise to get them out of the house for a few days after the burial.

There was another young couple on their honeymoon. They were Andy and Isabel, oblivious to the rest of the party. This was the couple that had been upgraded when Jules took their room next to Suzanne's. They would come to dinner and say "Good evening" to everyone and no one else existed for them afterwards. The look in his eyes was very profound and penetrating and when she looked at him her eyes were spellbound. They were both in their twenties, and you could tell they were more than just lovers, they were soulmates. It was as though they could read each other's thoughts and they would start laughing without crossing any words between them. Everyone at the table would look at them and smile. There were a total of twelve persons at their dinner table, including Suzanne and Jules.

After dinner, Mae invited them to join her at the Captain's party and Jules immediately said yes, but Suzanne hesitated, saying she was tired and had to get up early the next morning. Mae insisted and they attended the party and danced at Mae's insistence.

During the party the DJ played songs from the 80s. The young couple that sat next to them at the dinner table danced to the tunes of Saturday Night Fever and he—Andy—looked like John Travolta dancing. Everyone made a circle on the dance floor and applauded his sexy moves. They had a wonderful time that evening thanks to Mae's insistence. It was as though they had never parted. That evening they had a few drinks and laughed at Mae's outrageous behavior. Mae was so drunk she passed out and they took her to her room.

The rest of the evening they were talking about what they had done during the past twenty-five years. Suzanne danced with Jules and he just looked at her and smiled. She was in his arms and that was all he cared about. She hadn't changed. She was still very talkative, but more sophisticated. He just looked at her, she was so beautiful and he was thrilled as he danced with her very close and held her hand with his hand on her waist.

Suzanne was careful, after all they had left each other 25 years ago. She said to him, "Jules, it's strange to see you here. As far as I can remember you never liked cruise ships because they made you seasick. Are you here with someone?"

He responded that he was alone. When the party was over they walked outside to the promenade. She asked him again if he had come alone. Jules responded that he was there alone. Suzanne did not believe him. He asked if she had come with Mae, she responded "Yes," that she was her friend. She explained the cruise ship reservations were originally a second honeymoon for a friend and her husband. She found out she was pregnant and since she was nauseous all the time, gave the tickets to her. Mae insisted on joining her on the cruise ship and she finally gave in and said yes, but with separate rooms. "Now you know why I'm here Jules, but you haven't told me why you're here."

Suzanne kept insisting and asked again, if he was there with someone. When he responded that he was there alone, she was surprised and repeated sarcastically, "Alone?... You!" She asked again, "Jules, why are you here?"

He asked her why was she so interested in knowing if he was with someone and responded that he was vacationing just as she was and that he had followed the advice of some friends that had taken the same cruise ship the year before. She was not convinced with his response and did not insist anymore. She then asked why he had not joined them for dinner the night before and he explained the ordeal of the flight delay arriving in Athens. She asked again, "Are you sure you're here alone? Ok, it's very hard to believe that you are alone."

He nodded and simply looked into her eyes, held her shoulders until he saw his reflection in her eyes and could feel her heart and said, "I came here for you!"

She looked at him very nervously and said, "Repeat that for me."

She then reacted and said, "Impossible, we haven't seen each other for a very long time, try another line." She looked into his eyes, and closed her eyes. She knew that look very well and she was not going to fall for him again, and she said, "You are such a liar."

Jules responded, "I never lie when I'm serious about something."

"Well—she said—I don't believe you, don't answer the question."

Jules finally confessed that it was not a coincidence. He told her the truth that he had breakfast at the restaurant and ran into Layla and Andrea, and met her daughter Laura. She was very surprised and repeated, "You met my daughter Laura?"

He responded, "Yes," and asked why she was so surprised.

She asked, "Jules, why the sudden interest after 25 years. What did you expect, that I would be waiting for you? I have a life and plans for my future and I never entertained the idea that you would be in those plans. You are part of my past, not the present and certainly not the future." She then said, "Good night," and started walking towards her room.

At first Suzanne thought Jules was following her and was going to invite himself in. She asked him what his room number was and he responded by giving her his number. She looked at him and said, "How strange, that's next to my room. Your being here is a puzzle to me, we have staterooms next to each other, same dinner reservations, same dinner table, same cruise ship. I am wondering, what else do we have in common?"

He just smiled and opened the door to his room and said, "Good night," and walked in after she had closed the door to her room. All night long until they fell asleep they thought about each other.

Chapter Five

Day 3 - Sunday: Kuşadası

he next morning Jules called Suzanne and invited her to have breakfast with him. She accompanied him and they ate outside. The sun was shining, the day was beautiful, not a cloud in sight. The island of Kuşadası looked fascinating at a distance with its sandy white beaches and clear blue water. He asked her where she was scheduled to go for the day and she responded her trip was scheduled for 15:30.

He said, "Lucky me! I have identical activities scheduled."

Suzanne looked at him and said, "Well, Jules, I guess we will be seeing a lot of each other on the ship and on shore."

Jules did not respond, he just raised his eyebrows and smiled as though he was up to no good. Mae was still sick and did not join them for breakfast. She decided to stay in, have lunch and go straight to the boat that would take them to the shore where their land tours were scheduled.

It was Sunday, and they decided to take advantage of the morning and hired a guide for a walking tour before their tour at 15:30.

During the morning tour Suzanne had spoken to Jules about Mae. She said Mae was a very successful businesswoman, she was an only daughter and inherited a chain of hotels.

She dedicated her life to expand her business in Europe and Latin America and never settled down to marry and have children. She was a philanthropist and would donate money to further the education of students who did not have enough funds to continue their studies. David was one of those students and he was in the process of waiting for the results of his medical exam. He had actually met Mae while she was undergoing surgery in the hospital where he was doing his internship in his last year of med school.

He had been so kind to Mae, that for the first time in her life, she felt what it would have been to become a mother had she taken time to have a family and children. She learned that he was going to leave the internship for a time to help his parents financially. When Mae found out, she hired him as her assistant. He continued his internship and was able to help his family.

Mae invited him on this trip and asked him to make sure that she took all of her medications and did not drink too much. Although Mae seemed like she was drunk all the time, she really wasn't. She just liked to get attention and feel like she was the center of the universe. Last night was a little different, she was having too much fun and it seems she had an extra glass of vodka.

In the afternoon Suzanne and Jules arrived to meet their transportation for the tour. Mae looked at them and said very loudly, "What a happy couple, did you sleep together last night?" Suzanne told Mae she was incorrigible and she and Jules looked at Mae and smiled and shook their heads.

David volunteered to be the tour guide for the group. His grandparents were from Greece and he was versed in Greek history and language. He knew every detail about the Greek islands. As a child he would spend his summer vacation in Greece with his family and they would travel from island to island discovering the treasures of each site. David was tall with green eyes and black hair. He was very handsome and Mae loved him as if he were her son and enjoyed his company. She had helped him and his parents and he appreciated her kindness and generosity.

On this day, they were scheduled to take a tour to Kuşadasi. David started to read a little about the day's tour, which included a drive to the Temple of Artemis, which is one of the seven wonders of the ancient world, with a view of the Basilica of St. John, which was erected over his grave in the 6th century A.D. by Emperor Justinian.

They visited the Ancient City of Ephesus and explored Angora, Odeon, the Celsus Library, and the great theatre. It was definitely a must while in Turkey. After the tour, they were transferred back to the Izmir port for a free time to explore the island on their own.

Everyone on the tour was surprised at David's knowledge of Greece. He was viewed by some as a gigolo and as Mae's escort and not as the intelligent and professional man that he was. Suzanne, of course knew that Mae loved David as if he were the son she never had. Mae had told David's story to Suzanne and she also had gotten to know David very well afterwards. He used to work as a bartender and as a male stripper to pay for his studies and help his parents while going to school and during his internship. When he accompanied Mae to the pool, all eyes were on him for his muscle mass—like a body builder's. He would exercise every day at the gym and just put all the men to shame with his great body. Many of the women on the cruise started to exercise at the gym just to get a closer look at him. "What a waste—they would say—I wonder how much she's paying him." Some of the women would make comments about paying double or triple the amount, and Mae would walk by laughing out loud and say, "Eat your heart out girls, he's with someone." Mae didn't care what they thought. She was never going to see those women again after the cruise, they could talk all they wanted. She was not there to satisfy anyone's curiosity. Mae loved the gossip.

David followed Mae wherever she went. Mae would try to lose him and tell him to go on and have some fun on his own. David wouldn't hear of it and would simply tell her, "You're all the fun I want." He loved Mae's company, not only because of what she did for him and his family, but because of her caring and kindness. Beneath all her complaints and comments, he discovered a very lonely and loving woman who desperately needed a family and someone to love her and make her feel important and needed. All the money she had did not make up for the family she so desperately wanted.

David only saw a real loving woman hidden beneath all her complaints, yelling and demands when he met her at the hospital. All of the other interns did not want her case and he was assigned. From the moment he walked into her room he failed to see what the other interns had described as a witch. All he saw was what he wanted to see: a woman with a great heart who needed attention and someone to love. She was furious with the food and did not want to eat, pushed the tray and started cursing and yelling about the service. David left the room and she screamed louder. He promptly returned with a wheelchair and told her, "Get in. We're going for a ride to a very fancy restaurant." As she sat down he told her, "Buckle up, this is a fast moving vehicle," and he started racing in the hospital corridor, past patient rooms and labs and the nurses' counter. He would make screeching noises with his mouth and before stopping at the elevator started to whirl her around, got in the elevator and went to the cafeteria and ordered a sandwich and coffee for her.

All this time Mae was quiet. She ate her sandwich without complaining and she and David were just talking and laughing. The hospital director and David's supervisor came in to the lunchroom and started walking towards their table and David said, "Uh, oh, I'm in trouble, I should take you upstairs right away." He asked her, "Are you OK?"

As they approached the table the supervisor apologized for the incident and dismissed David and told him to wait for him in his office.

Mae said to David, "Don't you dare move from that seat—and, calling the director by his first name, warned—If you do anything to David you can bet your ass that you will not get the donation from me that you want for the new wing."

The director then smiled and said, "Of course, Mae," and told the supervisor to reassign David's duties to other interns.

Mae told the director that she only wanted David to be her intern while she remained at the hospital. David was released from many of his other rounds in the afternoon to have time for Mae. They had exciting conversations about hospitals and changes needed and service levels, and Mae talked about the similarities in service levels in hotels. They became friends.

After a few days David told her that after the following week he would be leaving, but said he found a wonderful replacement if she remained in the hospital. Mae was upset and insisted on knowing the reason for his leaving. David simply said it was a family matter he had to attend to. Mae respected his privacy, but once he left the room she called the director to find out why he was leaving. The director said it was confidential and could not reveal the information, but Mae would not take "confidentiality" as an answer.

The next day, when David went to visit her, she asked if he would come back to visit her when he left the hospital, and he said he had already made plans to do so. Mae asked about his replacement, and he introduced her to a wonderful intern, which Mae kindly accepted. After David left for the day, she called the intern and made conversation with her, and for two days she would ask her to return when David left.

On the third day of gaining her confidence she finally asked her why was David leaving. Of course she knew there was no "confidentiality" between friends. The intern told her that David was leaving because his parents found out and were ashamed that he was working in a strip club to help support them and his studies. David immediately quit his job and needed time to go job hunting and move back in with his parents, while saving enough money to return and finish his medical studies. Mae was heartbroken and teary eyed because David knew she was very rich and did not say a word to her. She then realized how honest and sincere he was.

Mae immediately called the director and met with him and said she now knew why David was leaving. They made a plan to have him continue his internship with a scholarship fund that already existed but had no funding. Mae donated money anonymously for students in similar circumstances. Of course it could not be so obvious for David to conclude that it was Mae's funding and they decided to grant five scholarships to different interns. They used the criteria in other scholarship funds and the staff's recommendations.

The next step was finding a job for David where he could have a flexible work schedule. When David was granted the scholarship he continued as an intern and he confessed to Mae that he had been granted a scholarship for his studies and told her the truth about his leaving. Mae acted very surprised and told him she was proud of his accomplishment.

Mae asked if he was working. He responded that he had just left his job and was job searching for a position with a flexible schedule to accommodate his work at the hospital. Mae said she was looking for an assistant, since it was difficult to find one, because she was so demanding, and wondered if he knew anyone interested. He said he had several friends he could recommend and would let her know.

Mae did not want him to know that she had created a new position for him and she had to figure out how to make him a job offer. It was a synch, she was so smart. On the following day she asked David if he could research some information on a piece of land she was interested in purchasing for a new hotel she wanted to build. She needed information on tourism, population, nearby hotels and their ratings. David said, "Sure, I'll be happy to get the information for you."

The following day, he had all of the information she had asked for. What was surprising was that she already had all of the research done by experts, but he added information on a new hospital which was being built with specialized services. He said it was a state of the art hospital and research facility and they expected to receive patients from all over the country. There was no hotel in that particular area, so there was a potential need for one. Mae asked if he had done this on his own and he said yes. She then decided to give him another assignment much more complicated than the first and again he returned the following day with all of the information she requested and more. She was upset with her management team that had taken a month to get her half of the information he had provided in a few hours.

Mae told him, "You know David, this is the type of information I need from an assistant, plus working out schedules for me, doing very minimal travel and of course having a good relationship. Do you think you would be interested in the job? It pays very well and you can work around your hospital schedule. What do you think?"

David was very surprised and said, "Well, it sounds like you have a new assistant, *Madam!*"

Mae started giving him assignments to verify work which had already been done by her staff. She finally left the hospital, and after returning to work reassigned her management team and only left those whom she knew were actually working and committed. She was back! David had his own office, but would mostly work from a computer Mae had given him.

He never discussed pay with Mae. When he received his first paycheck, he went to visit her personally and said they had made a mistake and paid him too much money. Mae looked at him and laughed, "I'm sorry we never discussed pay, but that's what my assistant makes."

David became teary eyed and told Mae, "No, this is too much money."

Mae responded that she paid employees four times as much for work they never did and it took them forever. He had done researh for her at a fraction of the time and for less pay. David kept insisting and said he could not accept the pay, that he would only accept half of what she paid him and that if she didn't have enough to pay him, he would work for free. Mae's tears rolled down her cheek and she said, "I am so thankful to God that I was hospitalized and that I have found the second most disinterested man in my life who is willing to work for free when I can pay triple the salary he is making."

The truth is he was making more money than the starting salary for a doctor, but he made Mae reduce the salary by half and continued to work for her after his internship ended.

There was a special bond between Mae and David, they both knew they were special to each other. The trip to Greece was the first trip they had taken together.

On this tour the group remained together. They had spent all afternoon enjoying the sites and laughing as though they had known each other for years. Mae had a comment for everything. She would just go on and on and the group did not get bored.

Mae commented to David that every moment that Jules and Suzanne shared would become an everlasting memory in the years to come. The present moment was their story, they were creating history together. They found unexpected treasures in each other, in the way they walked, talked, smiled, inhaled, exhaled, their fragrance, when they closed their eyes, or when the wind touched her hair and pushed it away from her shoulders.

Jules walked up to Suzanne and whispered in her ear that the sites were not nearly as beautiful as she is. Love had reawakened between them, they were young again and blind to their surroundings. As they walked, his hand touched hers, they both looked at each other as though no one else existed in the universe except for the two of them. They had picked up where they had left off years ago. When their hands touched they could sense how it produced all kinds of feelings of passion, of surrender that had been forgotten and hidden for years. They looked at each other with a profound look of love in their eyes. They were both mesmerized the rest of the day. He did not let go of her hand and always managed to keep her close. He didn't want the magic of the moment to end. He would look at her and a smile would brighten his face and his eyes closed and opened and smiled with a look of profound love. He felt as though he was breathing for the first time.

When they arrived at Izmir, Jules invited the group to have a light dinner at a restaurant the tour guide had recommended. There were several restaurants serving seafood and lamb or chicken souvlaki and great desserts. As they walked towards the restaurant there were vendors in the streets selling arts, crafts, jewelry and paintings of the port.

Suzanne stopped to look at the beautiful paintings. She wanted to buy one for herself and one for Laura. Jules was looking at the scarfs and he purchased one he knew she would like.

When they arrived at the ship it was late and they did not have dinner. Suzanne walked with Mae to her room and talked to her about Jules. She said, "He looks just as handsome from when I last saw him. His hair is grayer, but he is just as elegant and distinguished looking and as charming. There is something special about him that still keeps me captivated and turns heads when he walks into a room and, Mae, you were certainly not the exception when he arrived to dinner." Suzanne confessed to Mae that his presence made all of those feelings she had felt about him resurface and made her feel the long lost love from the past. She confessed she was beginning to enjoy spending time with him and to feel like she had been submerged in a pool of forgotten love.

Suzanne said she was just older and never thought about finding someone at this stage of her life. Mae sighed and said, "Honey, my mother used to say that age is just a number and she lived to 98 and had a Cuban lover who was younger. José was 85 years old. They used to dance together and go to dinner and have parties in the house and celebrate birthdays and anniversaries and any event you could think of. They slept in separate rooms, but were inseparable. As you get older, Suzanne, it's not so much the sex, but getting up with someone who tells you that you're beautiful and you hold hands, and spend your days together, watch TV shows, go to the movies or have a glass of wine together. You wake up in the morning to find you're loved and you hug each other and kiss each other because you're happy that you are sharing another day together. It becomes a habit, an attachment, the feeling that you cannot survive without the other. The other's presence, their companionship becomes part of you. You inhale and exhale the same air in the same room. The marriage vows represent this pure love or passion for the other, the words are not in vain, 'I, take thee, to be my wedded husband/wife, to have and to hold, from this day forward, for better, for worse, for richer, for poorer, in sickness and in health, to love and to cherish, till death do us part.' The power of love is so strong, that it attracts its soulmate even after years like it is happening to you and Jules. This is what 'until death do us part' means, our souls are united, inseparable, fulfilling and satisfying beyond words and understanding."

Mae continued, "I was too proud and lost at love. I regret not holding on to the only man that taught me the meaning of true love. I secretly loved him and never told him because I was ashamed of him. He worked in marketing at one of my hotels and because he was an employee I thought he was unworthy of me. He professed his love to me, but I didn't take him seriously and thought he was only after fame and my fortune.

One day he left and did not return, and I never knew anything else about him except for a farewell letter he wrote with no return address. In his letter he wrote that he had never loved anyone as he loved me. He wrote that he was strong enough to withstand my pride and insults, but not my lack of love for him.

"He could not understand why he loved me so much and I did not show any interest or affection. Everything he did was to surround me with love, patience, tolerance and kindness, until he felt all was lost and there was no reason for him to stay. His pain and sorrow had grown to the point that it was intolerable for him to stay and see me every day without my showing any interest in him.

"Suzanne, don't repeat my story of losing at love. I am a very lonely woman. I was in love with him and was very immature and spoiled and did not realize how much I loved him until after I lost him. Years passed and I even hired a private detective to find him and he was never ever able to find him, he had disappeared.

"Years later, while I was on a business trip in Chicago, I walked in to a shoe store and he was there purchasing shoes. I walked up to him and angrily demanded him to tell me why he had left me, why hadn't he called or returned. He just looked at me in disbelief and remained quiet and did not respond to my questions. Suddenly, a woman walked up to him and put her hand around his arm and asked him if everything was all right while looking at me. He looked at her and responded that everything was fine and introduced her as his wife. It took me by surprise, because I always imagined us finding each other and living happily ever after. I was infuriated that he had left me for that measly looking woman. I was not about to let her interfere in our lives now that I had found him and I was not about to lose him again. I immediately invited them over to dinner and he hesitated, but his wife insisted and we went to a restaurant and spoke all evening. I was still my usual conceited, egocentric, spoiled brat and found out he was unemployed. I jumped at the opportunity and said that I had a position at one of the Chicago hotels that he could interview for, but it would result in 75% of travel time to manage the worldwide hotel chain.

"His wife jumped at the prospect of employment and said it was a wonderful opportunity for him and she knew he would be great in the position. Little did she know that I would be waiting for him at all of his hotel visits. I would make sure our agenda would be identical. I was going to conquer this man, because she had taken him away from me and my mission was to get him back.

"The following morning I had him meet with personnel and he was hired. Afterwards we had lunch together in my suite, and I demanded that he tell me what happened. I did not realize how firm and resolute he was. He had made a decision to leave me years ago and his decision was final. It took him years to recover from me and he was happy and very much in love with his wife. He told me firmly that if he worked for me it would be strictly business and with no sentimental involvements or an affair. If I were to accept his conditions he would stay and work, if not, he would have no alternative but to leave again.

"He simply blew my mind, I couldn't let him go. I accepted his offer, but deep down I knew I would use everything within me to have him fall in love with me again. I stayed behind the scenes for about three weeks and he was doing an excellent job visiting the hotels and writing reports on improvements and recommending changes. He started a customer service survey and honors programs to recognize customer loyalty which have grown into monumental programs.

"This was the side of the man I had never bothered to know. He was intelligent, thoughtful, creative, brilliant and worked long hours. The hotel ratings were improving, we were merging with other business partners, business was booming and we started receiving awards for excellence in the industry. We started hiring more personnel, restoring the old with new softer pillows, colorful comforters, curtains, furniture. All of the growth went on for about two years, we had weekly business meetings and traveled a lot together.

"I respected his decision of keeping a strictly-business relationship and was happy just knowing that I would be able to speak to him and see him on an ongoing basis. One day we met at the Paris hotel and had a business meeting in my suite. We worked late that evening and had a working dinner. During the course of the evening something happened. Unexpectedly, while exchanging documents our hands touched and we looked at each other and put down our heads in embarrassment. He spoke first and said, 'I'm sorry, I didn't mean to,' and I interrupted and said, 'It's all right, you need not apologize.'

"We then looked at each other wanting to say so many things, I wanted to scream out and tell him that I loved him so much, his eyes were full of tears. For the first time in my life I felt grown up enough to know that if I didn't control my emotions at that moment and if we allowed our desire and animal instincts to take each other apart, we would have gained nothing and would lose everything we had built in our relationship. The respect and integrity we had developed was stronger than any secret moments of intense passion we could share that would destroy us, our relationship, and I would risk not ever seeing him again. All of these thoughts ran through my mind in seconds as we looked at each other intensely waiting for the other to make the first move. It was as though we made love with our eyes. I could feel him touching me, I could feel him inside of me. His presence was all over, we were spellbound. The moments were intense and overwhelming and finally he broke the silence and said, 'It's late, I think I should leave,' and I lowered my head with tears in my eyes and said nothing. As he opened and closed the door behind him, I knew we would never share the intensity of that moment ever again. That evening I realized how much he still loved me and how faithful he was to his wife.

"The following morning I sent him a message to start working early and when we met we never discussed what happened that evening again, it was as though it never happened. He is happily married with five kids. Can you imagine me with five kids? Impossible! Although many times I wonder how our lives would have been had I not wasted the first opportunity. A secret relationship would have been destructive for him, for me and for his wife which is a decent, loving person.

"One day, she and I had lunch together and she told me she had been jealous of me and thought I would interfere in their marriage. She said that when she met him he told her that he was in love with a woman who did not return his love and he would never forget her. She knew what she was up against: a memory, one to remember and the other to love. She had to gain his trust and love and she worked very hard for him to learn to appreciate her. Over the years his affection grew for her and it was enough for her to live with. She had settled for the little love he could give her and till this day she knows he has not forgotten his first love. He doesn't speak about it, but in his eyes he still loves that woman. She then told me, 'I later realized who the woman was' and with tears in her eyes said, 'I am so grateful to her for not destroying our marriage,' although she knew how much she loved him."

Mae had not realized that she knew. The three had made great sacrifices. She said, "Mae, I don't know how you have been able to work so close with him and hide your feelings, but your eyes and his always reveal the love hidden inside of both of you. I could not have been this strong, Mae, with someone I am in love with."

Mae was speechless, she hadn't realized she knew the truth and had kept silent. Mae then responded and said, "You are equally as strong, knowing the truth for all of these years, keeping quiet and not knowing if each night was the last. I could never have done what you have done to be silent and know there was someone else so close to him who could have jeopardized and destroyed your marriage."

She confessed that her love for her husband was how she was able to survive. The three of them had kept the same secret. Mae managed to tell her, "We have all been strong."

All she responded was, "He has two loves. It's been many years and I have silently loved him all of my life."

Mae's eyes were filled with tears, she had spoken from her heart and finally said, "Suzanne, take my advice, don't do what I did, keep him close and don't let him escape you. Till this day I have never married or had children. He is still here—pointing to her heart—I lost in love and I'm still paying the price.

"Lover boy looks very interested, he traveled this far for you and I would almost state he's fallen for you again and a little birdie told me he planned every activity to be with you. I also heard through the grapevine that the couple that was in the room next to yours was upgraded so that he could have the room next to yours. If you don't feel the same as he does, don't lead him on, but I think it's too late for that, you're hopelessly in love with the guy. So enjoy, make love and be happy."

"Mae—Suzanne said—this is 25 years later. I don't have the same body, and gravity has taken its course. Everything that was up is now down and everything that was down is now up, including my blood pressure."

"Dear, I would only be concerned about his gravity and there's Viagra for that."

Suzanne said, "Mae!"

Mae walked away with a mischievous grin and look in her eyes, raised her eyebrows and waving like a princess, said, "Enjoy."

When Suzanne left Mae's room, she and Jules saw each other and they both entered their rooms at the same time and said goodnight. Jules took a second look to wait and see if she would invite him in. Once in their rooms, they both leaned with their backs against the door. Both were breathing as though it was impossible to live without each other and they both turned to open the door and knock on each other's door and simply allow destiny to take its course.

When they opened the door and stepped outside they were both facing each other and he asked her if there was something wrong.

Suzanne said, "No, I was just..." and he invited her in to his room, which she quietly accepted.

He had ordered wine prior to inviting her over. His intentions were to spend a quiet evening with her without crowds or anyone to interrupt their moment. He just wanted to be alone with her. He knew that Suzanne did not drink in the past, but wanted the evening to flow with the same intensity as the day. When she walked in all he wanted was to feel her presence. They did not speak. In the silence their hearts spoke to each other as they looked into each other's eyes and all was said. They did not say any words, only their eyes spoke.

He then served a glass of wine and said, "For us."

Suzanne was silent. Jules told her he had purchased a gift for her at the bazaar. She was surprised, because she could not remember any moment when they were not together and did not expect anything. He walked around her seat and pulled her hair to the side and tied the scarf around her neck loosely. All of this was in complete silence. He kept his hands on her shoulders wanting to hold her tightly, but instead he turned and faced her. He simply looked at her and kissed her on the cheek, his hands were now holding her hair in the back of her head. Suzanne closed her eyes expecting more, she was ready for his next move. Jules held back, he knew that his next move would determine their future. He immediately stopped, his fears began to resurface again and he thought it better to wait and not ruin the moment.

They had already finished one bottle of wine. Suzanne was not used to drinking and she sat on the side of his bed while he opened another bottle of wine to serve her another glass. When he turned towards her she had laid back on his bed with her eyes shut. She had fallen asleep. Jules sat beside her contemplating her beauty. He was overwhelmed with the thought of her being in his room and in his life again. He kept repeating her name over and over again, "Suzanne, Suzanne." Her name was a familiar sound in his lips and it brought back many beautiful memories of the time when they were together.

When she woke it was still dark out. He had taken off her shoes and had covered her with a blanket. Suzanne looked at him and said, "I must have fallen asleep. Did something happen last night? I don't remember anything except having too much wine to drink. That is exactly why I don't drink."

He looked at her and smiled and raised his eyebrows as if to say something happened and said, "It was wonderful." He was a very bad liar and then admitted nothing happened. He laughed and said, "You just fell asleep and I looked at you all night long."

Suzanne said, "Jules, this is not right."

He said, "Don't say anything, let's just enjoy the moment and let things happen naturally."

They laid in bed looking at each other, and he took her hands in his. In their mind and heart there existed an unspoken language and a special bond so powerful and irresistible that it made them want to be together as lovers.

Although time had come between them, it felt strange being together because the years had passed by and at the same it felt good to be with each other. It was as though it was just yesterday they had said their goodbyes. They both felt so good about each other they didn't have to act as though they were meeting each other for the first time and wanted to impress one another. They were themselves, with all of the faults, insecurity and complications they had.

Suzanne then left to her room. All the rest of the night she wondered if this was truly happening. They fell asleep thinking about each other and desperately wanting for the sun to rise to be together again.

CHAPTER SIX

DAY 4 - MONDAY: SANTORINI

*E*ach day the cruise ship docked they would get up early just to see each other and spend time together, laughing, talking, enjoying each other's company. They were visiting all of the sites together taking in the beauty and picturesque scenery and enjoying the cruise. Suzanne loved to talk about her daughter and her studies and he talked about what he had done with the companies he had acquired. He had made a deal with his associate Bryan a very long time ago. Jules did not want to work full time and was not there on a full time basis. Bryan had passed and his son was doing an excellent job with the business and they maintained a very successful business relationship. Bryan's son had married and had five girls; they stopped looking for a baby boy after they had their last daughter. The girls had grown up and worked with their dad while they studied at the university and were smart business women. Only one of them was actually interested in the aircraft business and would follow after her dad's and grandad's footsteps. She had studied engineering, worked as an aircraft mechanic, had a pilot's license and was already designing her own aircraft.

Suzanne was impressed with the progress they had made in the industry. Jules's investment and his future with Suzanne was what made him decide to work with the company. When he spoke about the business with her he avoided the part about his relationship with her and simply talked about the good business decision he had made.

During their time on the tours and talking about their lives she realized that he seemed more secure about himself and not as serious and demanding of himself as before. He was different, he seemed more flexible and seemed to want to enjoy more of life.

She kept trying to ignore her feelings and did not want to admit to herself that his presence awakened long lost feelings as she had expressed to Mae. There was a force stronger than herself that attracted her to him like a mysterious stone or magnet. She would ask herself, if this could truly be happening, and even wondered if he was also feeling the same as she was. She even thought that they still had unfinished business from a prior existence that was responsible for pushing, pulling and attracting them together.

Suzanne was still confused as to why he said he came to the cruise ship when he found out she was there. She did not want to anticipate or entertain any ideas in her mind or get enthusiastic about him and think that he was really there for her. She kept pushing this idea from her mind. It was difficult for her to grasp this thought.

She could not stop thinking about him day and night. After giving it much thought it made her mentally exhausted and she decided to just follow Mae's advice and just enjoy herself, live the moment and not think about the future, only live in the present now.

That day their entire group left on their day trip to Santorini. They had heard so many wonderful things about the island that they were all looking forward to explore the beauty and treasures and the volcanic centre. David started to talk about Thira Santorini, which is a complex of islands called Cyclades.

Santorini is a small, circular group of volcanic islands located in the Aegean Sea, about 200 km southeast from the mainland of Greece. It is the largest island of a small, circular archipelago which bears the same name and is the remnant of a volcanic caldera. The municipality of Santorini includes the inhabited islands of Santorini and Therasia and the uninhabited islands of Nea Kameni, Palaia Kameni, Aspronisi, and Christiana.[1]

David explained that Santorini is essentially what remains after an enormous volcanic eruption that destroyed the earliest settlements on a formerly single island, and created the current geological caldera. A giant central, rectangular lagoon, which measures about 12 by 7 km, is surrounded by 300 m high steep cliffs on three sides. The main island slopes downward to the Aegean Sea. On the fourth side, the lagoon is separated from the sea by another much smaller island called Therasia; the lagoon is connected to the sea in two places, in the northwest and southwest. The depth of the caldera, at 400 m, makes it posible for any but the largest ships to anchor anywhere in the protected bay; there is also a fisherman's harbour at Vlychada, on the southwestern coast. The island's principal port is Athinias. The capital, Fira, clings to the top of the cliff looking down on the lagoon. The volcanic rocks present from the prior eruptions feature olivine and have a small presence of hornblende.[2]

---

[1] Thira-Santorini. (2016, Sept.). Thira Santorini. Retrieved from The history of Santorini - Thira: <www.visit-santorini.com/site/history.htm>.

[2] Bysshe Shelly, P. (2017). Greece secrets of the Past. Retrieved from

It is the most active volcanic centre in the South Aegean Volcanic Arc, though what remains today is chiefly a water-filled caldera. The region first became volcanically active around 3-4 million years ago, though volcanism on Thera began around 2 million years ago with the extrusion of dacitic lavas from vents around the Akrotiri.

The island is the site of one of the largest volcanic eruptions in recorded history: the Minoan eruption (sometimes called the Thera eruption), which occurred some 3,600 years ago, at the height of the Minoan civilization. The eruption left a large caldera surrounded by volcanic ash deposits hundreds of meters deep and may have led indirectly to the collapse of the Minoan civilization on the island of Crete, through a gigantic tsunami. Another popular theory holds that the Thera eruption is the source of the legend of Atlantis.[3]

The mention of Atlantis immediately caught everyone's attention. The group wanted David to talk more about the legend. David then started talking about the writing of the ancient Greek philosopher Plato and said had he not written so much truth about the human condition, his name would have been forgotten centuries ago.

"But one of his most famous stories—the cataclysmic destruction of the ancient civilization of Atlantis—is almost certainly false," he said.

Plato told the story of Atlantis around 360 B.C. The founders of Atlantis—he said—were half god and half human. They created a utopian civilization and became a great naval power. Their home was made up of concentric islands separated by wide moats and linked by a canal that penetrated to the center. The lush islands contained gold, silver, and other precious metals and supported an abundance of rare, exotic wildlife. There was a great capital city on the central island.

There are many theories about where Atlantis was, in the Mediterranean, off the coast of Spain, even under what is now Antarctica. "Pick a spot on the map, and someone has said that Atlantis was there," quoting, Charles Orser, curator of history at the New York State Museum in Albany. "It's every place you can imagine."

Plato said Atlantis existed about 9,000 years before his own time, and that its story had been passed down by poets, priests, and others. But Plato's writings about Atlantis are the only known records of its existence.

He said that few, if any, scientists think Atlantis actually existed. The National Geographic ocean explorer Robert Ballard, who discovered

---

<http://www.historymuseum.ca/cmc/exhibitions/civil/greece/gr1040e.shtml>.

[3] Alford, A. F. (2016, Sept.). The atlantis secret. Retrieved from <http://www.bibliotecapleyades.net/atlantida_mu/esp_atlantida_12.htm>.

the wreck of the *Titanic* in 1985, notes that "no Nobel laureates" have said that what Plato wrote about Atlantis is true.

Still, Ballard says, the legend of Atlantis is a "logical" one since cataclysmic floods and volcanic explosions have happened throughout history, including one event that had some similarities to the story of the destruction of Atlantis. About 3,600 years ago, a massive volcanic eruption devastated the island of Santorini in the Aegean Sea near Greece. At the time, a highly advanced society of Minoans lived on Santorini. The Minoan civilization disappeared suddenly at about the same time as the volcanic eruption.

But Ballard doesn't think Santorini was Atlantis, because the time of the eruption on that island doesn't coincide with when Plato said Atlantis was destroyed.

It is believed Plato created the story of Atlantis to convey some of his philosophical theories. "He was dealing with a number of issues, themes that run throughout his work," he says. "His ideas about divine versus human nature, ideal societies, and the gradual corruption of human society—these ideas are all found in many of his works. Atlantis was a different vehicle to get at some of his favorite themes."

The legend of Atlantis is a story about a moral, spiritual people who lived in a highly advanced, utopian civilization. But they became greedy, petty, and "morally bankrupt," and the gods "became angry because the people had lost their way and turned to immoral pursuits." As punishment, he says, the gods sent "one terrible night of fire and earthquakes" that caused Atlantis to sink into the sea.[4,5]

The group was fascinated by the story of Atlantis. Many of them thought it was a true story and were disappointed when David said that "Plato created the story to convey philosophical theories."

Their visit to Santorini included a visit to a Medieval Castle: Kasteli of Pyrgos. It is one of the five fortified settlements and the most important one. The rock was inhabited in medieval times, because the fortress offered protection from pirates.

The castle could only be entered from the "Porta", which obtruded a square structure with an opening at the bottom part from which the inhabitants of the castle could pour burning oil on invaders.[6]

Like all the other castles of Santorini, one can find a church close to

[4] Dyer, W. (2016). Atlantis—True Story or Cautionary Tale? Retrieved from National Geographic: <http://science.nationalgeographic.com/science/archaeology/atlantis/>.

[5] Alford, A. F. (2016, Sept.). The atlantis secret. Retrieved from <http://www.bibliotecapleyades.net/atlantida_mu/esp_atlantida_12.htm>.

[6] Kastrologos. (2017). Castles of Greece. Retrieved from Kasteli of Pyrgos: <http://www.kastra.eu/castleen.php?kastro=kallisti>.

the entrance. Below the castle there used to be a system of passageways, used for protection or even escape in times of need. Pyrgos became the capital of Santorini before Fira, which is the capital of Santorini today.

The first thing that you will see getting into the castle is in the church of Saint Theodosia, which is not the only one there. On the western side, is another church, "Isiodion" of Theotokos, which is believed to have been built in the 10th century and it has extremely valuable and historical icons and a wooden iconostasis! Finally the last church that he mentioned is the church of the Virgin Mary, which is located at the highest point of the castle and was built in the 1600s.[7]

David explained that the prophet Elias Monastery in Pyrgos is in a nearby village, on the top of the mountain of "Profitis Ilia's"; it is situated in a Monastery. It dates back to 1711 and its glory wielded great spiritual and financial power and considerable wealth. It even owned its own ship that conducted private business for the benefit of the monastery. At the same time, it was an active intellectual and patriotic influence. From 1806 to 1845 it ran a School where the Greek language and literature were taught.[8, 9]

David said that on our next tour we would visit Oia, a traditional village with charming houses in narrow streets, blue-domed churches, and sun-bathed verandas. Its streets have plenty of tourist shops, taverns, cafes, and other shops. He said, "The sensation of the first time you ever lay your eyes on this architectural gem—while looking at Rachel—is truly something to remember for life.

David had definitely fallen for Rachel. Everyone had become mesmerized at his beautiful descriptive words of Oia, which were meant for Rachel.

Their tour guide added Oia, located on the northern edge of Thira, built high up above sea level, sparkles like an adorned Mediterranean princess with no rival. Strolling around the traditional settlement is absolutely pure from noise and traffic, and one admires the wonderful creations of local goldsmiths, or have a dessert or a cocktail in an environment where effortless aesthetics delight. As time passes, your steps ritually lead you to the best view of the West, while indulging in the magic of the moment, as his Majesty the Sun disappears below the horizon,

---

[7] Geece, S. (2017). Amazing Castles and Fortresses of Santorini. Retrieved from Secret Greece: <http://www.secret-greece.com/amazing-castles-and-fortresses-santorini/>.

[8] Estia of Pyrgos Cultural Association. (2016). Retrieved from Secret Greece: <http://www.santorinipyrgos.com/prophet-elias-monastery>.

[9] Island, G. (2016, Sept.). Retrieved from The Greek Islands Specialist: <www.greeka.com/cyclades/santorini/santorini-churches/santorini-prophet-elias.htm>.

setting the waters and the skies of the Aegean on fire.[10]

Mae would only say, "Oh, my, how romantic; next time I will come with a date!"

During the tour through the monastery they spoke about the beautiful sights and Jules and Suzanne walked side by side. At one point they were sitting together and he told Suzanne to turn and look at a statue, and as she turned, he had tilted his head and they were so close to each other that their lips brushed and they just looked at each other. Suzanne's face reddened but she said nothing. As they walked through the village, there were different vendors selling arts and crafts, local souvenirs and handmade jewelry. He brought her a necklace and stood behind her, pushed her hair to the side and put the necklace on her neck. As he finished putting on the necklace he lowered his face and softly kissed her shoulder.

Suzanne opened her eyes in surprise, but was paralyzed and did not move. She did not know what to say or do, so he held her hand in his and led the way. She was numb not knowing how to react but followed his lead. Although her feelings were strong for him, she asked herself if it could be that she longed for love and hadn't realized it and maybe, just maybe, he arrived at a time where she was vulnerable and unsure of her emotions. From the moment she first saw him, she felt something for him. But, could this be love at this stage of her life, could she truly have found love again, and with "him" of all people. It seemed impossible, but it felt so good to feel alive and vibrant again and have her heart pulsating like the four-beat gait of a Paso Fino horse.

She silently fought with herself, even after deciding she would live the moment. Part of her just wanted to run up to him and let herself go, but part of her still felt the hurt, anguish and abandonment from the moment they said their goodbyes years ago. She had lost at love before and it was unbearable for her to think of repeating the same pain again. She could not understand how both feelings of love and pain could coexist and how she could still feel identical emotions resurface from their past.

When he held her hand she felt vibrant, full of newfound love and energy, and when he looked into her eyes, she realized the love she felt far outweighed the pain. Just being close to him walking side by side made her body vibrate. The new feelings were stronger and different than before. There was a greater sense of security and confidence. The doubts she had felt before were dissipating slowly. She felt she had conquered her fears and decided to let herself go and accept him and destiny.

---

[10] *Santorini Oia village.* (2017). Retrieved from in-santorini: <http://www.in-santorini.com/santorini-oia.html>.

She started reminding herself to enjoy his company and vowed that she would enjoy the rest of her vacation with him. Even if it meant not seeing him again when they arrived back home. Their time together at this moment would last her a lifetime.

Jules thought that after that kiss and holding hands, it would be easier for him to explain his feelings to her, but it was not as easily said than done. It was still difficult for him.

He sat down and contemplated how gracefully she moved as though walking on air. Suzanne had changed and looked better than ever. There was something different about her and he couldn't figure it out; she had the same beautiful long hair, she was sleek and slender, and she walked as though she was a model in a fashion runway. She had a bit of the old, mixed with what he discovered was a sense of self-sufficiency, self-confidence and a high self-esteem. She was no longer insecure about herself and her decision making. Ease and grace were the qualities she had learned. She had fulfilled her dreams throughout the years and she was comfortable with herself and with her achievements.

Her newly found self scared him because she was successful and she didn't seem to need anything or anyone in her life. She was content and for an instant he thought this would affect any future plans for them because she would feel that he would disrupt her peace and interrupt her work.

He still had not overcome his fears entirely. He was afraid of being rejected if he expressed his feelings. They were halfway through their vacation and he started getting desperate, he did not want to wait any longer. He longed for her to fall into his arms and to hold her close during the rest of their stay and confess the truth about not reaching out to her when she walked out and left him.

Suzanne had walked ahead to look at some souvenirs and Mae saw the loneliness in his eyes and held his hand to give him some words of wisdom and courage. She said, "I may be old but I can see a reflection of my own loneliness in your eyes. Don't do what I did. If you love her go after her." Mae didn't realize that by taking his hand, she had broken an intense moment of fear. Jules looked at her with a sigh of relief.

Jules confessed to Mae that he did not know how to piece things together. He now understood for the first time why it was difficult for him to work at building anything, it was the same with relationships. He never learned how to salvage any relationship including his two prior marriages, or with Suzanne, the woman he so loved. He let her leave without putting up an inch of struggle or just saying a word that would have changed their lives. He did not have the courage to turn the door-knob 25 years ago, run after her and ask her to stay .

Mae told him that Suzanne had revealed their story to her and she too was fearful of being hurt again, but decided that her love for him was so strong that she would take the risk of loving and losing again if she had to. Jules was encouraged by Mae's words knowing that Suzanne still had feelings for him.

Jules said that he found himself lost in unfamiliar territory again. He was trying to find a road that would lead him to make the right choices, but he hesitated at every turn, in every curve it made him stop and doubt. If he could just stop and continue and not feel fear.

He now found himself in the same situation he had lived 25 years before, and did not know what to do. He had never admitted to himself that he was afraid of being left alone, abandoned and rejected like his dad had done so many years ago. He had not realized until now that he still carried the pain and loss of his father's abandonment. He thought he had overcome the anger and fear he felt as time passed, but realized he never did overcome that feeling. He still felt his father's rejection in his heart and mind. He thought he had all the answers, but when he came face to face with reality, it made him realize he never learned to overcome his father's decision about him. Being destructive was his way of getting back at his father over and over again. Suzanne was part of the fear he had sustained for years. For the first time in his life he was coming to terms with his fear because he now realized it required a long-term commitment, dedication, devotion, and responsibility from his part. With Suzanne it meant faithfulness in a relationship which required family relations which his father had never taught him.

He always thought that crushing and destroying was what drove him, but it was the fear of losing that steered him away from what he wanted most. He was afraid to love and that's why he felt threatened by Suzanne. He feared losing her if he gave himself completely to her and that made him drive her away. He preferred for her to leave and not face the possibility of failure in the relationship because it reminded him of the feelings he had buried in his heart. He hadn't realized that the biggest failure was letting her go. He had taken a chance with Suzanne, but it had not worked because he did not try to hold her back. He now wanted to be with her because he loved her and he did not know where to begin the relationship and be successful. The damage his father had caused had to somehow be repaired and he knew that now. He wanted desperately for Suzanne's love to heal the wounds left by his father. It seemed so complicated at this stage of his life to not know how to get what he wanted. For the first time he had opened up and was at least able to talk about it and understand it himself, even if he didn't know how to mend it.

Mae told him, "Jules, Suzanne loves you and there is more to this love story than meets the eye and the untold truth will fill and overflow your heart with love and happiness for the rest of your life. She is also afraid, you will have to be strong for the two of you and once she realizes that you are there for her, she will respond. Jules, it takes courage, and if you don't put up a fight with yourself and battle your own feelings for what you want, you won't ever know how much you've lost and how much you have to gain."

He looked at Suzanne from a distance and she was laughing with some vendors and she turned to look at him and lifted up the object she was viewing so that he could see it and she smiled at him. All he thought about was wanting to spend the rest of his life with her. He took Mae's hand, placed it in his heart and said, "I really needed that," and whispered, "Thank you."

He walked right over to Suzanne and asked her, "Where have you been all my life," and she responded, "Waiting for you." He inhaled and exhaled with a sigh of relief. They continued shopping and walking while holding hands. Just holding her hand made him feel what he had not felt in a long time. He had forgotten what it was like to love again, to feel every inch of his body excited, exhilarating and electrified. He was in a trance. He was hypnotized by her.

When the tour came to an end, they sat down, and just as the tour guide had said, "they indulged in the magic of the moment, as his Majesty the Sun disappeared below the horizon, setting the waters and the skies of the Aegean on fire."[11, 12] What the tour guide had not said was that the magic of the moment was theirs, the majesty of the sun had set for them. He could not resist the temptation and turned to look into her eyes and he now understood the profound and penetrating look of the young couple at the dinner table. He now understood that it was much more than just being in love and making love. They were finally one person and he knew that he could not possibly live without her ever again. He finally spoke and told her, "Now I know what it means to take my breath away." They looked into each other's eyes and felt this was their moment, their time—breathless.

Could love truly be this good? It's indescribable. Jules said, "I feel I can't live without you, I can't live without looking into your eyes and closing my eyes at night and knowing that you are by my side and that I will wake up in the morning to find you there by my side."

Everyone started to leave and when the tour conductor announced that they were ready to leave, they did not hear him. He had to walk up

[11] Oia sunset. (2017). Retrieved from Oia-Santorini: <http://www.oia-santorini.net/oia-santorini-beaches.html>.

[12] Santorini Oia village. (2017). Retrieved from in-santorini: <http://www.in-santorini.com/santorini-oia.html>.

to them and say, "We're leaving." In the background everything became alive again. The conductor was telling everyone to get ready for their next spot on the tour.

Suzanne realized she had always loved Jules, but this time it was different. She felt the timing was ripe for their relationship, she had reached a level of confidence which made her very sure of herself. But there were too many things going on at the same time in her life. She was older, more mature, a soon-to-be grandmother. How could she have fallen in love now, too many years had gone by, and she was used to being alone. She knew that at some point in her life they would meet again, but never like this and not feeling as she did. How could she explain this to Laura and what would she say. It was too much for her to think about at this point and she just kept repeating to herself, "Enjoy! Enjoy! Enjoy!"

When they returned from the tour to the cruise ship, he walked with her to her room, placed her hand in his and, moving his face a little to the side, smiled, kissed her on the cheek and whispered, "How about if I pick you up for dinner in an hour?"

She looked at him, tilted her face to the side, opened her eyes wide and whispered, "I'll be waiting."

They both were dressed and ready before the hour was over. He had made dinner reservations at one of the restaurants so they could be alone. Jules insisted in sitting together and not across from each other at the dinner table. He had ordered wine and together they ordered dinner. As they drank wine, Jules started to ask Suzanne her plans once she arrived home. It was the first time he had mentioned the word "plan."

Suzanne said she and Laura were working on several business ventures. Laura was soon to take over the company and she would stay on as a consultant. Jules asked if she was dating anyone back home and she said, "Well that depends, why do you want to know?," and he said, "I asked first, don't respond to my question with another question." Suzanne said it was none of his business and started laughing as though she was making herself very important and unavailable.

Jules asked if she could see them together in the near future and Suzanne responded that she had not really thought about it, she was having fun and enjoying being together and had not entertained any thoughts about the future.

He asked her, "Why not?," and she responded that being on vacation was not real life but fun. Secondly, they had already tried and failed and they had separated a long time ago and the scars took a long time to heal. Thirdly, she was not ready to start a new relationship and have to cook and cater to someone, and lastly she was set in her ways. She said she felt it would change the direction of her life and she wasn't prepared to accept someone in her life. She was not as young as before. Jules simply said, "Well now I know you're not with anyone," raised his eyebrows, shook his head and smiled.

He then put his fingers in her face touching every facial line and said, "Suzanne you are beautiful, and every facial line represents an expression of you, an experience, every time you smiled and laughed and cried. Every line is what makes you who you are today, seasons passed, and the number of moments that took your breath way. We have to learn from trees and leaves that fall and flowers that wither, the spring makes a comeback and they bloom again, it's a rebirth. Life is continuous and does not cease. Some people wither like flowers and do not bloom again because they don't have enough love. They shut themselves inward and won't let anyone in and allow life to renew itself and take its course. You are like fine wine, you have grown better with the years. They say the older you get the better you look and you are more beautiful than ever."

Suzanne started to say something and he put his finger in her lips and said, "Don't say a word, just listen. Suzanne, age is just a number, who you are and how you feel is what made you who you were yesterday, and makes you who you are today, and tomorrow. Age does not matter, what matters is what you feel in your mind and in your heart. When I look at you, I don't look at age. I see a beautiful woman full of love, wisdom, beauty, harmony and balance who is at home with herself and does not pretend to be who she is not.

"You are the woman that I love!"

Suzanne could not believe what she was hearing, he finally said the magic words: "I love you." During the past few days, she had wondered why he came on the cruise and now she realized why. He had not forgotten her, she still held a special place in his heart.

Jules continued to talk and said, "Don't you see how our time is now. We are one man and one woman who have lived and laughed and cried and the experiences we shared are what has brought us here together today. I can't fix the past, I can only try to make the present whole, as I hope you would like to see it. What we build today is what will flourish and grow tomorrow. Let's not throw this away based on the past. Let's build a happier tomorrow, together, only looking back to see what we've accomplished and to give us strength for the future. All I know is I love you and that our story is not over, it has not been written. We will write it together."

"Jules, I have sat here silently, listening to every word you have said. It feels so wonderful to be here with you. In these few days we've been together, I have met a new Jules, a side of you I had never met before. This Jules is full of passion and reveals his feelings of love and romance. Looking at the past, I see a man that has matured and has learned to appreciate love, he is wiser and wants a second chance for love. Let's

enjoy life today, and see what tomorrow will bring and has in store for
us. If our time is ageless and timeless, we will know it. Just living for
today, we will have lived moments that will never be erased because
we have lived them and they have become part of our memories today,
tomorrow and always."

Jules heard her words and could not believe how she had changed
from the young woman he had met in a New York bar to the remarkable
woman sitting next to him. She did not cease to surprise him. "I have so
many fond memories of you and I remember how we met."

They were silent and Suzanne broke the silence and said, "Do you
remember how we first met?" Jules had just sipped some wine and he
immediately spit it out on the table and they both laughed out loud.

After dinner, as they walked back to their rooms, he invited her to
see an onboard show. They left together to the show and enjoyed it. It
was similar to a Vegas show. That night, when they walked back to their
rooms they both said goodnight while each was entering their room.

Back at the main dinner table everyone seemed to be tired and not
very talkative. Rachel's parents did not join them for dinner because her
mother was still feeling ill. When she arrived David could not take his
eyes off of her. She was dressed unlike all the other times they were at
dinner. She wore a cute short dress with a beautiful design, semi-high
heeled sandals and her hair was loose. Her beautiful skin was like a
porcelain doll, eyes blue like the ocean and when she walked all eyes
were on her. Mae looked at David and at the young girl and told him to
sit next to her, since she was going to the casino.

As Mae left, David told Rachel she looked beautiful and asked if
she wouldn't mind his sitting next to her. She responded by asking if his
grandmother wouldn't scold him and he said, "No, she wouldn't; sometimes looks can be very deceiving."

David said the name "Rachel" is a biblical name, and that he could
not understand how so much beauty could coexist in one person. He sat
next to her and she apologized and was embarrassed at her inappropriate
comment. He responded there was no harm done. Rachel told him how
impressed she was with his knowledge of Greek history and wanted to
know how he had learned so much about Greece. He told her that his
family was from Greece and he vacationed here every summer. He had
also taken a course and learned about Greek art, museums, castles and
monasteries, and philosophers. There were other areas they had not
visited which included archeological sites.

He spoke about the day trip to Santorini, Santa Irene, Stroggylis,
Kallisti, and Thira. A land that has been constantly inhabited ever since
prehistoric times. He told her he enjoyed the visits to Akrotiri, which
was located on the southern edge of the island, where there was an

impressive excavation site.

The archaeological hole unearthed the secrets of daily life in the pre-historic civilization of Thira, so closely related to the Minoan, where time stood still when the 1600 B.C. great volcanic eruptions occurred. Close to ancient Akrotiri there is a settlement, a village of serene beauty crowned by its Venetian castle. There is also the temple dedicated to the Virgin Mary, the *Panagia Episkopi in Exo Gonia*. It was built in the 11th century by Alexios I' Komninos, and is an important meso-byzantine monument.

They also visited the Ancient Thira in Kamari / Mesa Vouno. Santorini's city of historic times, a fortress built at an altitude of 385 m., which was founded in the 9th century B.C. by the Dorians and traces can be detected of inhabitation up to byzantine times.[13]

He mentioned the Museum of Prehistoric Thira in Fira. The Museum is the home of Akrotiri murals and mobile findings as well as of artifacts from other areas that date back to Neolithic times. He spoke to her about the Winery country. The unique soil composition of Santorini's land, a true volcanic gift, combined with the microclimate conditions of low rainfall but high humidity, are the canvas on which the local vine varieties such as Asyrtiko, Nyhteri, and Vinsanto can express their best qualities.

Rachel was truly impressed by all of his knowledge and did not think badly of him and Mae. He talked on and on about Santorini consisting of an entirely volcanic rock formations and invited her to the Preveli beach the following day in Crete. He told her about the different beaches, the Black Beach, in Kamari, watched over by a huge rock, a fairytale of black sand unfolding. Its wild beauty captures the eye, in perfect contrast to the peace and openness of the eastern horizon. As we move to the south along the coastline, we arrive at Perissa, where the heart of intense beach-life beats, with plenty of activities, beach bars and restaurants to choose from.[14]

David spoke about the different beaches they had not visited and described each one. The Red Beach was a magnificent geological forma-tion, a bright red sandy bay in the embrace of huge volcanic rocks, located in Akrotiri which are destined to mesmerize you. He said the White Beach was accessible by boat departing from Akrotiri. "An unparalleled natural beauty like yourself—he said to Rachel—where ice-like formations of white rocks with pale blue hues, like your eyes, reflect the light inviting

---

[13] *Prehistoric Thera Museum - Fira Santorini.* (2017). Retrieved from fira-san-torini: <http://www.fira-santorini.com/prehistoric-thera-museum.html>.

[14] *Santorini beaches.* (2017). Retrieved from in-santorini: <http://www.in-santorini.com/santorini_beach.html>.

you to dive into Paradise."[15]

By the end of the evening they had talked about all of Greece, and finally Mae had come up looking for him. Rachel told him that his grandmamma had come to pick him up to tuck her into bed. He did not appreciate her remark. He excused himself and simply said, "Duty calls," and left. She again hated herself for making such a stupid remark. He was fascinating and she enjoyed his company and conversation.

Mae realized what was going on and stayed behind a few minutes. She asked Rachel if David had told her that he was a medical student and her personal assistant. Mae was not one to explain anything or satisfy anyone's curiosity, but she felt it was crucial to defend David. "Rachel, he is accompanying me while he awaits his medical exam results. I cannot travel alone and he helps me with my medication."

Rachel responded that he hadn't said anything about himself or Mae. Mae told her, "He is a gentleman, and a gentleman never tells. But don't underestimate him." She winked at Rachel and walked away.

That evening, after dinner, Jules and Suzanne went back to their rooms, he put a bracelet he had purchased for her in a box and sent it to her with one of the porters. Suzanne sent him a note saying, "Thank you for the gift, it's beautiful." He then sent her a bouquet of red roses, thinking she would surely come to his room, but she sent another note thanking him for the roses. He waited and she did not come. That night they were both restless.

Jules left his room and went to the casino and Suzanne left her room and sat under the stars in one of the lounge chairs in the deck. When Jules left the casino he also walked outside and saw Suzanne and asked if the seat next to hers was taken and she said, "Well they are available except for this one, it's reserved for a man I met."

Jules said, "Well, he must be a very lucky guy to sit next to such a beautiful woman as yourself."

He laid down next to her to watch the stars and the glittering and sparkling sea with the reflection of the full moon. It was a beautiful evening with the silence of the ocean, the soft breeze in the calm summer night at the corner of the earth. All you could hear was the movement of the ship as it cut through the ocean and the waves splashed against the ship. They were there all alone in the middle of the big ocean and no soul in sight to witness their romance.

They looked at each other and smiled, and as he leaned over to kiss her, all of a sudden it started pouring rain, and as they got up to leave, the door that led to the inside was locked and they had to find another

[15] *Santorini beaches*. (2017). Retrieved from in-santorini: <http://www.in-santorini.com/santorini_beach.html>.

entrance. As they ran, Jules grabbed Suzanne by her arm and looked at her intensely and pulled her against his body and kissed her. She kissed him back and he said, "I should have never let you go. I have always needed you," and she looked at him and said, "Then, why didn't you ever come after me, why didn't you come and tell me you loved me, why did you deprive me of your love for so long. Don't even say you love me, you're lying and I don't want to be hurt by you again. I thought I had taken you out from here," and she touched her heart with the palm of her hand.

She continued, "It took me years to get over you and you suddenly make a comeback in my life as though we just left each other yesterday and expect me to start loving you again. You can't expect me to react as though 25 years did not separate us."

"Suzanne, I don't want you to start loving me again, I want you to search deep down in your heart and find the love we shared. I found it, it's here and I love you more now than ever. A thousand years could have separated us and our love would have survived." A tear is rolling down his cheek as he says, "I love you, I have always loved you. Let me be that man in your life you thought you had lost. Give me an opportunity, even if you feel you have given me an opportunity and lost. Please, Suzanne, don't fight your feelings, the love never left, don't leave me," and he grabs her and kisses her romantically and passionately. The rain is still pouring down on both of them and he says, "The pain of losing you again is unbearable."

Suzanne tells him, "I don't want to love you, it hurts me to love you and I don't want the pain, the hurt after every encounter. Part of me screams to have you hold me and never let me go and part of me is fearful of being hurt. Don't you understand it's painful to love you? Please leave me, don't start what you know you can't finish. Jules please just go."

"Please don't give up on me, walk with me, run with me. It's not too late, we can do this together."

"I can't help you, you need to do this on your own, and you need to know what it is that you want. I can't guide you. I waited for you to come back and you didn't, you never came back for me."

"I know, I didn't know how. All I know is that I don't want to lose you again."

They just stood there in the rain looking at each other and they put their arms around each other and kissed passionately.

Jules said, "I can't let you go, I need you, I love you. I didn't know how to tell you that I loved you. I was so afraid you'd turn your back on me some day. I know your pain, I have felt it. I never knew how to reach out and say 'come back.' I'm sorry, I'm sorry, I'm just not that strong, help me and stay. I'm not going to let you go," and he grabbed her face and looked into her dark eyes. "When you left the first time I was afraid. I was more afraid of not being myself, of not having self-control. You controlled me with your love. It was too much for me, I preferred to let you go for fear that if I loved you too much you would one day leave me. When I found you again, I realized that the love far outweighed the fear, I am strong enough to face my fears now. I have never loved anyone like I love you. You take my breath away, will you rescue me?"

Suzanne took a deep breath and said, "You have never left my heart, it was difficult for me not to give away my feelings, my surrendering to you. I too am afraid that we will leave each other again. It was too painful for me and I can't go through this a second time. I would not survive. I have always loved you. I was trying to be strong pushing you away and not shedding a tear when you were near me."

Jules kissed her and said, "Your love drives me insane. I want you to wake up next to me every morning, I want to feel your body next to mine and I want us to feel like we are one. I want to look into your eyes every morning and enjoy your presence. Is it too much to ask? Is there not enough love? I want to sweep you off your feet and tell you every day that you complete me."

Suzanne tried to push him away and he said, "Suzanne, don't distance yourself from me. I realize that I should have held you back, we could have had children and grandchildren together, yours and mine, ours. All I have to show for my life are my assets with no family or friends. I should have continued the life we started together, but I panicked. You went on to have the daughter that could have been ours. I wish we hadn't left each other. Let's give *us* a try."

As he spoke, he wouldn't let her go, he touched her wet hair, her face and her arms. He held her shoulders and put his arms around her. He was holding on to her. They were both soaked and he would not let her go and he held her face and kissed her again and again. They finally started walking together and found an entrance and with her hand in his, they walked back to their rooms. She went to her room and when he tried to follow her in, she said, "Good night, Jules, we will see each other tomorrow morning," and she closed the door behind her. Jules returned to his room frustrated and angry, but he would not give up on her. Tomorrow was another day.

Suzanne was hopelessly in love with him again. How could she have refused him? She had already discussed her feelings with Mae and had decided to accept him. It was confusing for her to go back and forth aimlessly with so many uncertainties. It drained her emotionally and made her sick. She was heartbroken because of what had just happened between them and because she had not told him the truth about what happened when thy broke up 25 years ago. Tears were rolling down her cheeks in desperation. She would have never thought of finding him, or him finding her now! It was too long ago. It wasn't difficult to explain what had happened to her. She knew she loved him, but there was still that dark cloud in her mind that kept reminding her to be careful and not step into pain.

She tried calling Mae, but David said she was sleeping. David realized how desperate she was and said, "I will be right over."

When he arrived Suzanne was still crying. David asked what had happened and she told him that she couldn't tell Jules how much she still loved him and about Laura. How could she now reveal... David interrupted her and said, "I know, but you need to tell him the truth. You simply can't start this relationship after so many years without his knowing the past."

Suzanne calmed down after a while and she told David, "I can't tell him, I don't dare."

David said, "The truth hurts but if he truly loves you, he will understand what both you and Laura tried to tell him."

Suzanne said, "No! I first need to know if he truly wants to be with me or if his feelings will end when we dock."

Jules was returning from the bar with a drink in hand. He was restless and could not sleep. All night he kept thinking about what had happened when he held her in his arms. She had kissed him back, she could not deny the feelings she felt for him. It was now his turn to help her face her fears of the past, present and future.

As David opened the door to leave, Jules looked at David angrily and demanded to know, "Why are you leaving Suzanne's room at this time?"

David looked at him and simply said, "I suggest you not give any thought to what you think just happened or are imagining and just devote your attention to a woman who loves you, is confused and doesn't know how to interpret her feelings. You have a history together, events you both shared and situations which joined you for life which you are oblivious to." It was time for him to know, but it was not David's responsibility to tell him.

Jules knocked on Suzanne's door and when she opened the door thinking it was David, she said, "Don't say a word!"

When she saw it was Jules, he said, "I won't," and they walked towards each other, hugged each other and she whispered, "I love you." This moment was theirs. He then left to his room and she soon fell asleep.

CHAPTER SEVEN

DAY 5 - TUESDAY: CRETE

*T*oday they were anxiously waiting for the morning to see each other. Last night certainly was special, she had finally revealed her feelings. He knocked on her door and asked if she was ready for breakfast and she opened the door with a big smile and said, "I'm ready." A new adventure was in store for them on the land tour. Today they had planned to visit Crete to go scuba diving or visit the sites. There was a scuba diving experience which was a one day course for everyone and no previous diving experience was required.

The young married couple, Andy and Isabel, wanted to go scuba diving with David and Rachel, but her mother wouldn't allow it. David accompanied Rachel. Her mother was still sea sick and had not recovered. She was sorry her mother was sick, but was happy with the time she was spending with David.

Suzanne was not interested in scuba diving, she wanted to explore Crete on an adventure of an extreme off-road Land Rover safari. She would have never done this back home, but she felt adventurous. The tour included stunning gorges and plateaus only accessible by 4WD vehicles, passing through remote villages, and a stop for a refreshing swim at Preveli Beach. Once off the road and out into the wilderness of southwest Crete on this safari, it was full of beautiful scenery, stunning mountains and remote beaches. The driver would navigate the difficult terrain, taking the group to places which seemed inaccessible to other vehicles, while the tour guide spoke about Cretan culture.[16]

The day started with a drive through the wilderness, up to high altitudes, where they had views of the magnificent gorges. There were vultures and eagles high above and they passed through small traditional

---

[16] Guide, G.Y. (2017). *Crete: Jeep Safari*. Retrieved from <https://www.getyourguide.com/heraklion-11806/crete-jeep-safari-to-preveli-beach-t57797/?referrer_view_id=277890bc0a81cb99e11d89135be23698&referrer_view_position=5>.

villages full of character, and made a brief stop for coffee at a remote mountain village.

Back in the vehicle, they drove through the mountains to the village of Spili, famous for its spring water. Located under the shadow of Mount Vorizi, the village has a Venetian fountain with a row of more than 25 lion heads supplying cold mountain water all year round. They walked around the small shops selling handmade souvenirs and traditional handicrafts. Suzanne took beautiful pictures and bought bracelets for Laura and jewelry that she knew she would love and clothing for her unborn grandchild.[17]

The late afternoon trip was driving along dirt tracks and bumpy roads through more villages, where time stood still. Passing Kerame, they enjoyed panoramic views of the southern Cretan coast and the Libyan Sea. The views were so beautiful all you could hear was the clicking of cameras. People taking selfies of themselves and with their families with the panoramic views in the background. The view was so beautiful they wanted to remain stranded in this island. When they arrived at Preveli beach they stopped for a swim to wash off the dirt and dust. Preveli is one of the most beautiful beaches on Crete, and was chosen by Bacardi as an ideal location for its TV advertisements. The beach was decorated with tall palm trees and beautiful coasting crystal clear water, it was the only beach in Crete where you can swim in cold mountain water or ocean water in the same place.[18]

They walked back and stopped for a traditional Cretan meal with wine. After lunch they continued to drive into the mountains for more vivid scenery, and more photos as they were taken through the stunning Gorge of Kroustaliotico. Suzanne and Jules were taking in the sites. It was so romantic to be enjoying this tour together. They were displaying their love to everyone. Even Andy and Isabel commented on how beautiful and in love they looked during lunch. Andy said that he wanted to look at Isabel when he was older in the same way that Jules was looking at Suzanne. Everyone in the tour became silent and just observed how the two of them looked so romantic; you could feel their love spreading like a wave in the ocean. Their love was contagious.

As they headed back towards the dock, they were at a mountain top and there was a magnificent view of the city of Rethymno. The group agreed this was one of the most beautiful tours they had taken. They also agreed that driving along dirt tracks and bumpy roads was quite an adventure.

---

[17] Ibid.

[18] Crete, S.C. (2016). *Prevei route - Safari club Crete*. Retrieved from <https:// safariclub.gr/product/preveli-route/>.

When they arrived to the ship, Suzanne ran to her room to prepare for the evening. She dressed exquisitely for dinner. She wanted to look beautiful because Jules made her feel young, alive and she was enjoying his company as in the past. This time it was different, the feeling was different. David's pep talk helped her let go of those negative thoughts she was experiencing and Jules words made her feel like she was walking on air. There was a greater degree of confidence in herself, which had been lost when they separated because of his lack of commitment. Suzanne tried to talk to him about the past, but he avoided any unhappy conversations which would lead them away from the loving mode they were enjoying.

During dinner, Mae was very philosophical and started to distinguish the difference between love and confidence. She said that both go hand in hand. She explained that you can love someone because our hearts never stop loving. Love can withstand all trials and tribulations.

But confidence is different and does not depend on love. Confidence in a relationship is trust, loyalty, faithfulness; it's an oath, a pledge. When confidence is lost all is lost because confidence and love go hand in hand, and when destroyed, relationships fall apart and die

Love is the pledge in marriage vows "to have and to hold, from this day forward, for better, for worse, for richer, for poorer, in sickness and in health, until death do us part." The vow is of love, confidence, concern and mutual support for one another. One expects that the one you love will always be there for you and when they fail to be there or the love is threatened and destroyed the confidence losses its strength. Mae said, "I was not there to nourish most of my relationships when I was younger and I now realize how important it was to be there and be supportive. I took everything for granted because I loved and lost because I was... oh, well, I guess it's that time of the month when I get sad."

Well, everyone wondered what was wrong with Mae this evening and the couples thought about what she had said. They had never really thought about it, but agreed that it did make sense. David gave an example of how a couple could lose confidence but not love. He said, "If one of them is unfaithful to the other and they are forgiven and remain together, the love is there, but the confidence is lost. When you hear the expression, 'I will forgive, but never forget,' it's the love that forgives, but the betrayed confidence does not forget."

Suzanne said quietly to Jules that the loss of confidence existed because, as she had said to him last night, he never came back for her. Jules responded that it wasn't true, that he did come back and tried to reach her and she was gone.

That conversation did not go well and Jules started talking about the beautiful panoramic views in Crete. He took her hand and said, "Let's just forget the past and look only to the future and what we have found in each other."

He said he was very happy to be there with her and having the opportunity to have gone together to Crete. They were living and creating a love story as time went by. They could have never imagined how beautiful it was being together and enjoying each other's company.

Afterwards, they walked together to their rooms and Suzanne said goodnight. He kissed her goodnight and stalled to see if she would ask him in. He walked over to her and put her hand in his heart and said, "This piece of equipment is dancing and pounding and rejoicing for you. I did not see this coming, you have made me come alive again and I want to look forward to waking up in the morning just to see you and be with you. It's difficult to breath without you. I know you feel the same. I can sense that our feelings are mutual."

Suzanne closed her eyes and said, "I know, I know."

She walked into her room, bit her lip and closed the door behind her. He walked to his room and looked back to see if she would open the door, but she didn't.

Later that evening he sent her a different gift with a note thanking her for the wonderful day they had spent together. He sent her a gold necklace with a heart locket and a key in a small box. When she saw the gift, she put her hand on her face, she blushed, touched her lips and smiled. Her heart was pounding and she wanted to see him. She was breathless. She closed her eyes and started to reach for the door when she heard a knock on the door. She felt paralyzed and closed her eyes. She knew it was him standing behind the door. What would she say, what was he expecting?

He knocked a second time and started talking behind the door and he told her, "I know you're there, I know you can hear me. I know that you feel just as afraid as I am. It's not too late, let's give us a chance. I don't know what will happen tomorrow or the next day, all I know is today I want you more than I ever have. I want to scream to the winds," and she opened the door and he continued talking and said, "I love you, I was stupid to let you go. The only thing I know, is that I love you, today, tomorrow and forever after. I know you feel the same. I can feel it in my heart and can see it in your eyes." He finally said, "Suzanne, I'm afraid too, we can do this together."

Suzanne had tears in her eyes and as she stands there he walks towards her and she starts to say something and he put his finger in her lips, pulled her hair to the side and kissed her neck and her shoulder and slowly worked his way to her cheeks, eyes and mouth. He had slowly removed the straps from her night gown until it fell on the floor and they laid down together and made love. After a while she had her head on his arm and they both started talking at the same time.

He asked, "Suzanne what happened to us? I am so complete with you. I don't ever want to let you go." He sat up and said, "You're not married, are you?"

She laughed and said, "Noooo!, Jules I'm not, are you?"

"No!"

That night they made love again as though they would never see each other again. They didn't talk, there was only the sound of the wind and the ocean. He told her, "I hadn't realized how much I loved you and still love you more than ever and this time I don't want to lose you. I want us to stay together."

She simply smiled and said, "After all these years, Jules, I don't know what power has brought us together."

That night they stayed up and talked, and he asked her about Laura's father. He told her what Layla had said about him and she said that's not exactly what happened. He had not run off with her assistant.

Suzanne started to tell him about their relationship and how she met him. He was taking several classes at the university when they met and started spending time together reviewing class notes and studying for exams. He was brilliant and would explain and help her understand and apply the different concepts.

They started dating and afterward she discovered he was very ill. He had not spoken to his father for many years and blamed him for his mother's death. When he became ill he forgave his father and told him about his disease. His father never left his side, he had lost his wife and now he was also going to lose his only son.

"His father wanted his son to be happy and proposed that we should get married. I was surprised, but Michael thought it would be a good idea and I accepted, because we had Laura to raise. He wanted to give Michael all the happiness he could while he was still alive. I accompanied Michael throughout his illnesses, hospitalizations, recovery and care.

"At some point I had left school to care for Michael and he was not happy with my decision.

"He was such a fine person that I wanted to make sure his last years were peaceful and happy. He was in remission for about five years and we continued our studies and after graduation his father helped us open up a business.

"After about a year he became sick again and did not want to burden me by giving up my work to take care of him. He decided to run off with my assistant so that I would become angry with him and not leave my work. I later realized it was a plan for me not to fall behind in our business and not miss him terribly when he passed on. When he died he left me his inheritance which came as a complete surprise to me. I had some funds I had saved through the years and I then started to follow all of your investments, and purchased stock where you invested and became very rich. I continued to open other accounting companies. My father in law had very good friends with huge corporations and they started to give me some of their business. The company continued to grow and we eventually merged with other smaller companies.

"My daughter continued her studies and followed in her father's footsteps."

She suddenly stopped and couldn't continue the conversation. She looked at him wanting to tell him the rest of the story, but she was afraid.

"Jules, I know it's late, but I have to talk to you about Laura and our company."

As she started talking to Jules he dozed off and she couldn't continue the conversation. She stayed up a while, thinking how difficult this conversation would be and she soon fell asleep in his arms.

Next morning they ordered breakfast, and while they waited for breakfast he went to his room to get some clothes and he looked at himself in the mirror, looked down and said, "What a stallion." He then lifted his arms like a body builder and twisted and turned his body to show off his physique. "Wow, you still have it, kid!"

Suzanne was still lying in bed face up with her hair spread all over her pillow and thinking about the night and what just happened. She was laughing by herself and she covered her face with the sheets wanting to hide. She was definitely in love all over again. She took a quick shower and dressed for the tour. When he returned, they had breakfast and were both laying down facing the ceiling. He told Suzanne that he needed some energy tabs if he was going to survive the next two days on the ship.

Suzanne responded, "We've only just begun," and jumped on top of him laughing and said, "We are making up for 25 years of lost time." They both laughed.

It felt so good to be laughing and just being herself with an old friend.

CHAPTER EIGHT

DAY 6 - WEDNESDAY: RHODES AND SYMI

After breakfast, they left together to go on the tour to Rhodes. They had heard such wonderful things about the island, but were still undecided if they would join the group for the trip to Symi in the evening.

When they arrived at the boat, Mae was her usual self with her bold personality and asked what had happened to them in the morning, since they didn't make it to breakfast. Suzanne responded that they had the flu.

Mae laughed out loud and said, "The flu?, what an interesting new name, is that what they call it now? I'll have to use that some time."

She continued to ask questions, and asked, "Well did you both have the flu? Or was it just one of you? Did you call a doctor?"

Suzanne and Jules remained quiet, looked at each other and just laughed. The rest of the group that heard the conversation were trying to control their laughter and after a few seconds they all exploded in laughter.

All Mae could say was, "Hummff!"

The tour began with a beautiful drive along the East coast of Rhodes, heading to a village called Lindos. After arriving at Lindos, they had a chance to take a donkey taxi up to the Acropolis of Lindos. They had never taken a donkey taxi and the children on the tour were especially excited and they all wanted to take the first ride. Afterwards, they had spare time to spend in the village's shops.[19]

Acropolis was beautiful with the most beautiful breathtaking view. During this tour he had purchased a butterfly and had planned to buy her a ring he saw on the ship and put the ring in a box inside of the butterfly to give it to her. He was going to ask Suzanne to marry him. He didn't want to lose her this time and he did not want to be without her. After much thought he decided to wait until they arrived and pop the question.

---

[19] *Lindos.* (2017). Retrieved from The most common form of transportation is the Donkey!: <http://www.lindoseye.com/transport.htm>.

They had decided not to join the group to Symi. Richard started to read the information about the island until their tour conductor arrived. He said the island is one of the southern islands off the west coast of Turkey. It is a small island just north of Rhodes and it is a popular destination because of its picturesque port and the Parnormitis Monastery.[20]

Symi was once famous for its wooden shipbuilding and for its sponges; now it relies almost entirely on tourism. Trees have disappeared from much of the island and sponges have vanished from its waters. Symi is a small island with a population concentrated in the port resort of Gialos where dozens of ferries tie up daily. Paved roads lead to a few beaches and the rest of the island is laced with rough tracks and mule paths. Taxi boats provide services to the more remote beaches, otherwise they can only be reached by a trek over the hills.[21]

By this day everyone in their group was talking to each other, sharing photos and taking group photos. Isabel took photos of everything. She had become the group photographer. This tour ended late that evening. When they arrived to the cruise ship, everyone dispersed and went to their rooms or to have a late evening snack.

That night after dinner Suzanne and Jules went to his room and they slept together and woke up looking into each other's eyes. He told her, "Every time I look in your eyes I get lost in your eyes and every romantic phrase comes into my mind that I want to tell you. I want to see myself in your reflection and I want you to close your eyes and record my presence and my love in your eyes, and in here—pointing to her heart—and here—pointing to her head—. Because you are in here—pointing to his heart—and in here—pointing to his head—. Now I know the feeling and understand every love poem that has ever been written. Thank you, Suzanne, for being in my life and for letting me feel what I have never felt before. No man should ever die without having his heart rejoicing and dancing to the tune of love."

As they looked at each other, he raised her hand to his face and kissed her hand and she started to touch the side of his head and his hair and touched his lips. As she touched his lips with her hand his lips separated as they continued to look at each other. They both knew what they wanted from each other and he pulled her over to him and they made love and fell asleep in each other's arms.

---

[20] *Panormitis Monastery*. (2017). Retrieved from The Greek Island Specialist: <http://www.greeka.com/dodecanese/simi/simi-churches/panormitis-monastery.htm>.

[21] *Simi History*. (2017). Retrieved from The Greek Island Specialist: <http://www.greeka.com/dodecanese/simi/simi-history.htm>.

CHAPTER NINE

DAY 7 - THURSDAY: CHIOS AND MYKONOS

*T*hey were up early and wanted to go on this trip. It was their last visit before returning home the next morning. There was one tour in the morning and another during the evening.

After breakfast, they joined the group on the tour to Chios. The tour conductor gave a briefing and said the island lives off tourism to a certain extent, but it is not their major source of income. One of the island's most important resources is mastic, from which you make chewing gum, and others live off fishing, farming or working on the ships.[22]

According to Greek history of Chios, this is where Homer was born and lived sometime around the 8th century B.C. Of course, there are many more islands that claim the same, and since we don't even know if he was an actual person, the speculating is a bit in vain. There is a stone on the island called Homer's stone (Petra Omirou), where the poet sat and worked according to those that believe he was from here.[23]

The name of the island comes from the Greek word for snow, 'Chioni,' since the island's patron god Poseidon was born under snowfall. During ancient years the island was quite wealthy because of its mastic and wine, and this was also the first place in Greece where they had slavery. Chios fought alongside Athens against the Persians in the 5th century B.C., and was later to be ruled by Macedonians, Romans, Venetians and Turks. It was during the Turkish rule that the island suffered one of the worst massacres in Greece. Because the island had been forced to revolt, the Turks punished it by setting an example: killing 25,000 and enslaving the rest. This brutal destruction of the island touched many European personalities of the literature and art such as Victor Hugo and Eugene Delacroix, who painted the famous painting of the massacre of

---

[22] *Chios Mastic.* (2017). Retrieved from The Greek Islands Specialist: <http://www.greeka.com/eastern_aegean/chios/chios-products/chios-mas>.

[23] *Chios.* (2017). Retrieved from in2greece: <http://www.in2greece.com/english/places/summer/islands/chios.htm>.

Chios that is now in the Louvre Museum in Paris.[24]

Mykonos was a walking tour, there was time to explore the streets of the most fabulous island of the Aegean streets and experience the true beauty of Mykonos. They went on the evening tour with their friends. By that time Andy and Isabel were friends with David and Rachel and they had planned to go together. Rachel was interested in knowing information about Suzanne and Jules, it fascinated her see how they were so deeply in love with each other and she wondered if they had known each other from before. The three of them looked at David, because he knew her and all he said was, yes, they had met before.

Suzanne and Jules went on the tour. It seemed as though they had been there for a long time. After the morning tour had ended they went back to the ship for a late lunch with Mae. They stayed with Mae a while, and Mae decided not to go on the last tour. She had told David to spend time with Rachel. Mae had approached Rachel's parents about David and they were impressed with him and allowed their daughter to spend time with him.

Jules confessed to Mae that he had taken her advice and was very happy with his decision and with Suzanne. She said, "Jules, she is a smart girl and there are still many things in the past which will be a part of your future that you will need to discuss. You never called or looked for her and she had to make decisions on her own."

Jules looked puzzled and asked, "What decisions?" Suzanne was returning to the table and interrupted their conversation. Mae and Jules did not have another opportunity to speak again because they were all leaving the next morning.

That night, when they arrived, Suzanne returned to her room to pack and after a while she had taken a shower and was wrapped in a towel when Jules knocked on the door. She put on a robe and he said he wanted to talk to her before they arrived home. Jules started to speak to her but Suzanne had unlocked such a passion that he could not resist the temptation of holding her. He stood behind her and started to pull on the robe. He started kissing her neck and her shoulders and started touching her neck and her back and slowly removed the robe. She turned to look at him and they began to kiss again as he laid her down and touched her body. She began to put her head back, close her eyes and enjoy what he was doing to her. She then laid beside him and he was caressing her hair.

That night they slept together and woke up in the morning. Jules said, "This is how I want to wake up with you every morning, in my arms and looking into your eyes and making love to you every single day."

Suzanne looked at him and thought how happy she had been with him these past few days. It had been years since she had been with anyone

---

[24] Ibid.

and it felt so good to love and to be loved. He awakened every passion in her body and he knew exactly where to touch her to make her desire to be with him.

76

CHAPTER TEN

DAY 8 - FRIDAY: ATHENS

The ship had already docked when they woke up. He left to his room in the morning and she showered and was ready to leave. As they were leaving their rooms, he grabbed her in the corridor and started to caress her hair and kiss her passionately. They wanted more, they simply had not had enough of each other and they laughed and left together.

He had turned off his phone on the cruise ship and refused to take any calls, all he wanted was to enjoy Suzanne, relax and take in the sites. This had been the first uninterrupted real vacation he had ever taken.

But when he decided to turn it on again as they got off the cruise ship in Athens, he started to receive phone calls from his attorneys about scheduling negotiation meetings with a company he had offered to buy. The lawsuit he had filed was pending, but the judge ordered the parties to meet and reach an agreement and a trial date had been scheduled in the event they were not able to negotiate.

He continued to receive numerous calls and would turn around smiling at Suzanne and asking her to wait, that he was almost finished. She knew this scenario all too well. History was repeating itself. This was Jules.

The wait finally took its toll. She had waited more than two hours and when he turned his back to her she waived a cab and left. She was gone. He was still in the middle of an important call when he turned around and saw she was gone. He put his hand down with the telephone in hand, closed his eyes, shook his head and continued talking on the phone. When he finished the conversation and hung up the phone to call her, he realized he did not have her phone number. He called his secretary to get her phone; he called the restaurant and it was closed. He didn't even have an address for her. Where was she, what did he do! He just sat there and the calls kept coming in and he didn't answer any of the calls. How could he have put his calls and his business before her again?

They had different flight reservations returning back home. When he finally arrived in New York he was able to get her phone number and called her every day for two months and told her he had one final business deal pending, in addition to the lawsuit. He wanted to wrap up these final details and did not want any loose ends in the future. Every day he would tell her how close he was to meeting with the head of the company whom he wanted to negotiate with. The company and its executives would not even grant him a meeting and he was growing impatient.

Jules was very happy with his success in the final negotiations of the lawsuit. He had conceded to end the ordeal. He did not receive the amount he had anticipated. It was certainly a very generous amount, but less than he was expecting. His attorneys convinced him that the negotiation was by far better than going before a judge who could decide differently. In the end he had won because, as the saying goes, "a bird in the hand is worth two in the bush."

The settlement was published in all of the newspapers without disclosing the confidential amount agreed upon, but speculation into the amount by the media was very high.

Every editor wanted to do a cover story on the millionaire bachelor. He was on the cover of several magazines and he loved the attention he was receiving. He was invited to parties and the reporters would publish different articles about women, romance and love. He had become the most eligible bachelor, playboy "Jewels." Everywhere he went he was surrounded by beautiful women wanting to be the next Mrs. "Jewels." All of the attention he received and the women who threw themselves at him did not interest him. He only wanted the love of one woman and he was angry with himself again for not giving Suzanne the attention he had vowed on the cruise.

When he walked into his apartment in the city at night without the day's glory and praise and the parties had finished, he realized how lonely he was. He had all of the success and everything that money could buy, but no one to share it with, no one to enjoy his success with him. He did not have a family waiting for him to come home to, have dinner and talk about the day's events. All he had to show for his success in the evening was a cold turkey sandwich in a brown bag. His success did not compensate the emptiness of the apartment and his lonely life. He was a changed man.

He thought about Suzanne and how lucky she was to have a daughter. The family he could have had with her, but failed because he was afraid of losing. It was pathetic to feel success in business and be so unsuccessful in relationships.

His past fears only drove him to where he was today, a very lonely man without a family and without true love and happiness. He called

Suzanne that night and her voice mail came on. He realized she was not taking his calls and he deserved her not wanting to speak to him or be with him. He had ruined their relationship. He was such a coward he didn't even leave a message.

Suzanne saw his name and number, and was tempted to call, but she had already given up on him and did not call him back.

As soon as he hung up the phone he left to go to her apartment. He was desperate to see her. When he arrived, the doorman would not let him in until he called Suzanne. When he called her, she said that he was drunk and not to let him in. Jules threatened the doorman and he allowed him to go upstairs.

Jules knocked on the door and Suzanne called the doorman to ask him why he had let him in. The doorman responded that if he didn't let him in, he threatened to buy the building in the morning and the first thing he would do was fire him.

Suzanne opened the door and Jules said, "I'm so lonely without you."

She just looked at him and said, "You can sleep on the couch, I have an early morning meeting."

He asked if they could talk and she said, "NO! Good night."

In morning she woke up to the smell of coffee, he had laid down next to her and when she opened her eyes, he was looking at her. Suzanne told him, "You are impossible!"

He ignored her comment and responded, "Isn't it wonderful to have somebody wake up next to you, make you breakfast in the morning and serve you coffee."

She got up to take a shower and locked the bathroom door behind her. When he went to open the door and found it locked he said, "Suzanne don't you trust me?," and started laughing and she screamed, "GO AWAY!"

Suzanne got dressed, had breakfast with him and they both left to work. Jules asked her where her company was located to pick her up for lunch, but she declined to answer. He then invited her to dinner that evening and she said she had a date. Jules asked with whom, but she did not respond and stepped into the cab. Jules also sat in the cab with her. He insisted on knowing who her date was and she told him to leave her alone and to please leave the cab. He said he was not leaving until she told him and she said, "It's a date with my daughter." He then smiled and left the cab. When he left she scoffed loudly.

Chapter Eleven

Chapter Eleven

Return to Reality

*T*hat same day, a reporter received anonymous information that Jules had been with a mysterious woman on a love boat in Greece. Reporters started speculating about the woman and who she was. They also received a picture of the woman with her back towards the camera. Suzanne immediately called Mae and said, "Tell me this isn't you talking to the reporters."

Mae said, "Suzanne, dear, what on earth are you talking about."

Suzanne said, "Don't play innocent with me Mae, I know you very well and this sounds like a Mae thing."

Mae acted surprised and said, "Suzanne, why are you accusing me, I'm your friend."

Suzanne said, "Exactly!" and hung up the phone.

Suzanne was furious with Mae and afraid that someone may have taken a picture of her and Jules. She did not want any kind of publicity. She had already decided not to take any more calls from him and that did not deter him from showing up at her apartment. How could she have entertained the idea that he was sincere? He had started calling her every day for two months and when the publicity started the calls started dropping off, it seemed as though he had forgotten her.

She could not get him off of her mind day and night. She then decided to start working again with her daughter Laura. Her business was very successful and it would help her stop thinking so much about him and she could help Laura who was tired and sleepy all the time.

As she sat in her office, she started thinking about the two years she had spent with Jules. She would listen to his conversations on business decisions, stock purchases and investments. She learned his strategies and would make decisions based on what she had learned from him. She would often ask herself, what would Jules do in this case? She had obtained a business degree and would read the financial news and books which eventually made her very successful in her business. Jules did not know much about her company and didn't know the magnitude of her business. She was very discreet in running her business and would not grant interviews and avoided having her picture taken. She kept her late husband's last name and appeared under the name of S. Collins.

Jules had heard about the success of the company, not knowing it was hers. He had instructed his staff to provide him with information and they had been researching the company for over a year. He had started investigating her when he discovered the company he sued was under a confidential investigation by the Security Exchange Commission. He then put Suzanne's company on hold, while he addressed the issues surrounding the lawsuit.

He knew the company was solid and U.S. based with some international exposure. His interest was to *expand* it further in international markets.

Suzanne was not interested in selling company stock to an outsider. Her attorneys were approached expressing the interest of a confidential investor in her company. She had given it some thought only because she and Laura wanted to focus on expanding their international operations. She had dedicated her time to build the company for herself and her daughter. She had thought about selling, but Laura was not in agreement. Suzanne then decided not to sell her share of stock and would not sell even if it meant remaining a wholly domestic company.

Suzanne and Laura both knew that in order to keep their competitive advantage they had to grow. One of the strategies was to hire someone with a strong strategic background on international markets, with impeccable integrity, and an eye for innovative financial and marketing strategies. They both looked at each other and started laughing, they knew there was only one man that could do it all.

The second plan was tied into the first. They already knew who the confidential investor was. Laura contacted the company and scheduled a meeting to discuss their offer. The meeting was scheduled for a week later. It was Jules who was interested in buying them out and they finally developed the courage to schedule a meeting.

The meeting was scheduled for 9:00 am and Jules arrived very early for what he and his staff thought was going to be a showdown. Jules had all of the strategies in place and he sat with his staff feeling very confident and waited for the company's staff to arrive and commence negotiations.

They were all seated at the long oval shaped conference table made of cherry wood, with two conference telephones at each end. There was room for 20 persons in the conference table. Suzanne knew it was Jules who was interested and remembered his mentioning wanting to invest and buy out the company stockholders. She had realized he was talking about her company. She had her assistant distribute a prospectus of all company assets both domestic and some international information on investments and the stockholders. The room was filled with all of the board members from the company, attorneys, financial analyst, comptroller, and heads of different departments in addition to Jules's staff. There were only two empty seats, reserved for the President and the CEO of the company. The CEO was the first person to walk into the room.

She introduced herself and welcomed everyone in the room and expressed her sincere interest in having a successful meeting. Jules looked at her and told his attorney that he thought he had seen her before. He said, "She resembles the waitress I met in the café called Rush Hour." He looked at her and was dumbfounded. He remembered that Layla had said that she was Suzanne's daughter. But he thought, "No, it's impossible, although the resemblance is remarkable."

She then walked up to Jules, shook his hand and said, "Do you remember me, Mr. Quinn."

Before he could respond, a tall, thin woman in a grey suit walked in, with her hair stylishly combed in a bun. She looked stunning. She came into the room and as she sat at the head of the table she welcomed everyone and apologized for being late.

Everyone from Jules's team dropped their jaws: Jules was in awe. Suzanne continued to speak about the company and outlined the morning's agenda. Jules was speechless, he finally realized that Suzanne was the president of this prestigious company that he wanted to buy. He finally recovered his composure, stood up and asked that everyone except Suzanne please leave the room. Suzanne's staff remained seated and he said, "Everyone."

Suzanne looked at her staff and shook her head in agreement with his request and looked at her daughter and said, "It's OK."

Suzanne remained seated at the head of the table and Jules leaned his back on the conference table, crossed one arm and held his chin with the other hand.

When everyone had left, they were silent and he walked up to her and she told him, "I tried to tell you Jules, you didn't listen."

Jules said, "Suzanne how it is that you're the president of this company. You knew all along and didn't say anything to me."

Suzanne said, "This is the business I inherited after my husband's passing. My father in law was so depressed after having lost his wife and his only son that he did not want to work another day. He left all of his shares to Laura and to me. I had inherited the majority of company stock when Michael passed away. I kept investing wisely every cent.

"With the money I had saved and I received from you I gave Laura a very good education and sent her to private schools and college.

"I started investing in your companies and continued working this company with my late husband about 22 years ago. I continued to work under my late husband's name. The man I married did not leave me, he died and I kept his name for business purposes, that's why you never found out who the real owner was. I knew that at some point we would meet again and here we are. After we broke up, I went back to school and gave myself a chance for success.

"I obtained a MA in finance as well as my daughter Laura. I never thought it would take these many years for us to meet again, and when I least expected it. Destiny bought us back together again. I want you to know that this business is ours, the stock holders are Laura, me and you. You own 30% of the stock under Laura's name, she has 30% and I own the rest of the stock."

"Suzanne, do you mean to tell me that I own part of the company I wanted to buy. Why do I have to find this out now?"

"If you would have returned my calls, but you never did."

"How can you say I never returned your calls? I called you many times. Someone had given me your new number. After so many unsuccessful tries to contact you I thought that you didn't want to speak or hear from me again. It's true, I needed some time to resolve my personal problems before we could have been together, but it didn't take too long to resolve. I looked for you, I tried to track you down to no avail."

"Jules, it seems you are still resolving those issues. It would have never worked out between us, not then and not now."

Jules said, "Twenty five years ago, I missed you when we broke up. I was devastated. It was a feeling I was all too familiar with, but nothing in my life prepared me for what I experienced when I lost you. I realized too late that I was afraid of loving you so much, because you had changed me. I loved you so much I felt I couldn't breathe without you. It was a feeling I had never felt before. When you left, I preferred to lose you. I learned too late that I was struggling with my fears of the past in the present. It was too much for me to bear and when I couldn't find you all I did was absorb myself in my work, but all I thought about was you. I have never loved anyone like I have loved you, and it scared me. I preferred to lose you than to feel the way I did. Suzanne, it's not easy for me to admit that I think of you day and night, that I wake up thinking about you and that you are my last thought when I go to sleep at night. I don't like to feel that I'm not in control."

Suzanne angrily said, "I never received any of your calls. I was lost because you never even bothered to call and ask how I was. Jules, I thought about you all the time. I thought you didn't return my calls because you didn't love me anymore and I simply stopped calling. I was afraid that you would think that Laura was an excuse for you to stay with me and love me. I could not endure the thought of holding you back and have you make a commitment because you felt responsible for us. I didn't know what to think anymore. I was hurt and angry and I buried you deeply in my heart and tried to forget you."

"Suzanne, what are you saying? What did you mean when you said that Laura would have been an excuse?"

"Jules, I wrote you to tell you about Laura and sent you baby pictures until she was five. Someone used to send me money in your name for Laura. I realized in the cruise ship that you did not have a clue about Laura when you mentioned you had met her. When you didn't return my calls and never asked to see her, I simply thought and decided it was of no use to keep trying to let you know anything else about our daughter."

Jules said, "Wait, wait, wait," putting up his hand, for her to hold that thought while he called his secretary. He asked her if he had ever received phone calls and letters from Suzanne when she left.

The secretary responded, "Why, yes, Mr. Quinn. Suzanne sent you many letters and called many times."

Jules asked, "How come you never gave me the messages or letters."

"Mr. Quinn, your assistant told me that you were very angry with Suzanne and he told me bad things about her. He instructed that I should never mention her to you again. All of the correspondence and messages were given to him, because he said it was to avoid you further pain and anguish. I did as he requested, sir."

Jules became so angry and he called his assistant in and asked him, "John, did you know that Suzanne was pregnant and that she gave birth to my daughter?"

John did not know how to respond and said that whatever he did was to avoid him further pain. "I witnessed your suffering when she left. You had stopped working and started drinking and I did this for your own good."

Jules asked him, "Did it ever occur to you that I would find out the truth."

John responded that Suzanne disappeared and he had lost all contact with her and he would send her money for Laura at her last address. After a while the mail was returned to him. He then was afraid to tell him and as the years went by it grew more difficult for him to say the truth. "When I realized I was wrong, it was too late. I'm deeply sorry, when I saw the three of you together today I was relieved because the truth would be revealed."

"John, how could you have been so selfish, you know more than anyone else how much I wanted a family and how much I loved Suzanne. Laura is my daughter. She is the CEO of this company, she is the child that your selfishness took away from me. John, you were like the brother I never had. How could you have deprived me of my own child?

"I want you to go through that door and never come back, never call me or try to contact me again. I never, ever want to see you for as long as I live. The damage you have caused is beyond description and is unforgiveable."

"But Jules—John insisted—this was for your own good. Suzanne had changed you, and she had transformed you into another person. It was for your own good."

Jules said, "Please leave, I don't want to end up in jail, just go!"

After John left, Suzanne called Laura and asked her to come in.

Suzanne said, "Laura, in all my life I have never kept secrets from you. When you were a little girl I told you all about your father and you have always known who he is. Unfortunately, as we found out today, your father did not know that he had a daughter. So, Laura, I would like to introduce you to your father, and Jules, I would like to introduce you to your daughter, Laura.

There were tears in all of their eyes. Jules was the first one to speak.

He said, "Laura, when we first met, I looked into your eyes and there was something so special about them. When you looked at me and tried to conceal your emotions, I immediately felt a bond between the two of us, even though I did not have any idea of who you were. I felt as though we knew each other all of our lives. Now I understand why you were so surprised and could hardly speak when our eyes met and you were so quiet and could not respond to my questions on the menu."

Laura said, "I realized who you were when you spoke to me. I had never seen you in person. I had read a lot about you in the papers and kept pictures I would cut out from the newspaper articles. I have to say you're not a stranger to me. I know all about you."

Jules asked, "Why didn't you ever come to see me, call me?"

"Mom tried and there was never a response. I tried and you never called back. We both decided to leave things as they were and knew that one day we would meet and here we are at a business venture. Time has finally caught up with us.

"You know, it's kind of nice to finally meet you and get to know you. You really are not any different than from how mom described you."

Jules shook his head and said, "Really, how did she describe me?"

"She described you as being smart, having charisma and good-looks and its really wonderful to finally meet you. I have been looking forward to meeting you for the past 24 years, Mr. Quinn, or should I call you dad?"

Jules's tears were rolling down his cheeks as he put his arms around Laura and told her how fortunate he was to have her in his life and to be able to say that he has a child and that he is a dad.

"All of a sudden I wake up to the fact that I am a dad and realize how wonderful it is to have a family.

"Laura, tell me about yourself, talk to me about you. I want to know everything about you. What did you do when you discovered the relationship between us and I want to know what you have done for the past 24 years? Just looking at you, I know your mom has done an outstanding job in raising you."

"Do you mean, when I discovered you were my father?"

"Yes! I want to know every detail."

"When I was a little girl, I grew up knowing another man as my father. When Michael passed away I was about seven years old and when I was about 12 years old, I found pictures of you and mom tucked away in an old purse and letters addressed to you in envelopes that mom had never sent you. When I asked mom, she told me all about you and that you were my dad. As I grew up I saw you in the newspapers and I used to ask mom why you never came to visit me. Mom used to say that we would meet sometime in the future. As I grew up she told me that you never responded to her letters and phone calls. I started to hate you. I became very rebellious and went to see you one day to ask you why you didn't care about me and your friend John stopped me from seeing you. He said you were going to be so happy to see me, but you were out of town. He asked me for my phone number and said he was going to plan a surprise visit. I waited and waited and you never called. When I saw him today he didn't even recognize me. I really dislike that man for not letting me meet you," Laura said, with tears rolling down her cheeks.

She continued, "I then hated the two of you. As time passed, I left you a dozen messages and you never responded, now I know why. One day John met with me and said that I was only interested in your money and he gave me a check for me to go away and never come back again. I became so angry that it drove me to finish school and become a financial wiz just like you. I wanted to teach you that I didn't need your money, that I was just as smart.

"When we stepped outside, while you spoke to my mom, John asked to speak to me and confessed that you didn't know anything about me, that it was he who drove me away from you. Destiny has a way of putting the pieces together where they belong and after so much anger for years, he finally disarmed me. The hate I had felt for years just left when he told me you didn't know about me. I feel as though I have just removed thousands of pounds of anger off my shoulders, though I am still very angry with him because he deprived me of you."

"Laura, I am so sorry, but I am going to make it up to you. We will spend time together as a family to make up for all of those lost years. I am here to stay, my main purpose in life is now to be your dad, spend time with you, and if your mother will allow me, with the two of you. I feel as though all of my life I have been preparing for this moment, please accept me. I will make both of you so happy.

"Let's have dinner this evening at my house and we can start catching up. You know all about me and now I want to know all about you.

"When I first saw you, you were working as a waitress and now you're the CEO of this company, what happened?"

"Well, I have to start off by telling you that I am married. My husband, his name is Richard, is a chef. We met in college and mom helped us open up the café. The business has been so successful he has opened up about 12 more in different cities and they are working out just fine. Richard and I are expecting our first child, so I have to tell you that you are soon to be a grandfather. I think you need to get over the first shock of being a dad and work through the part where you will be a granddad."

"This is too much excitement for one day. And I am also going to be a husband if Suzanne will have me. Now I've become a father and a grandfather to be. I didn't see this coming." He closed his eyes and said, "I want to celebrate with my family."

Jules then told Suzanne, "I'm so sorry, I didn't know. I was not successful in my family life. In all of my work and success, I never took the time to build a family. Tell me it's not too late, tell me that we can do this together."

Suzanne looked up at him and smiled and said, "All my life I waited for you. When I saw you in the ship, I didn't know what to think or to expect of you. All of the pain and suffering disappeared. The love that I had felt for you resurfaced and I couldn't think, my heart overflowed with a feeling so powerful, so strong it was overwhelming. I felt young again and my body felt so irresistibly attracted to you that I just let myself go. It didn't matter if you would leave again, all that mattered was that we were there together, I felt time had not passed. I loved you over and over again. My heart screamed out to you and I felt your heart pounding and I knew it was our moment.

"But when we docked in Athens and you started taking all of your calls, reality finally set in and I realized then that you were still the same old Jules, nothing had changed, and everything was the same as when we left each other so many years ago.

"I was so frustrated, Jules, you made my life and my feelings fall apart again. I let you into my life and you destroyed all of the love I gave you. For the past two months I waited and nothing happened. We are here today because it's business. This is your decision and I have made mine. I'm sorry, I have to leave now, Laura can make all of the business decisions, she has my vote of confidence. I trust her judgment. Goodbye Jules."

"Suzanne, where are you going? I'm here, you have made me the happiest man in the world, I'm here and I love you. I don't only have you, I have a family. I don't want anything else anymore. I have found what I've always wanted. Suzanne, I love you with more than just my heart. I love breathing the same air with you, our hearts blending together. I love holding your hand and holding you in my arms. I love caressing your hair and we now have a daughter. Something you and I created, she is us, Suzanne."

"No Jules, I have always had a daughter. Now you have a daughter."

"I want to spend time with her, I want to know all about her and be with you."

"Jules, I think it's nice that you want to spend time with Laura, but I will be leaving. We are not a couple. I want you to understand that you made that decision, not me! Goodbye."

Chapter Twelve

Aloneness

*L*ater that evening, Laura and her husband visited Jules in his New York apartment. Suzanne was still very angry and decided not to go.

Jules and Richard got along so well. It was as though they had known each other for years. They talked about the restaurant business and how successful the business had become. Jules started talking about the menu and recommended different meals and ideas on expanding the business. Laura then interrupted and said, "This is family night, no more talk about business."

Jules responded, "You're right, I guess I'm just postponing a conversation about Suzanne and why she is so angry. I don't blame her, I got carried away as usual when I arrived in New York. I did not devote the time she needed after leaving the cruise. I'm not sure she will ever forgive me, but I will do whatever it takes to get her back."

Jules showed them pictures of his house in upstate New York and asked them to move in with him. He said there's plenty of room for them and the baby. He insisted that the baby should grow up away from the city life and not in an apartment.

Laura laughed and said, "You sound just like a dad and grandfather, but it's too soon to make decisions because of the closeness of our apartment to work. We can discuss this later."

Jules asked Laura for advice on Suzanne. He tried calling her several times and she hadn't returned his calls.

Laura said, "I can't get involved, that's between the two of you. I know how to pick my battles and this truly is not one."

After a few days Laura and Jules met every day to talk about themselves, the company, the family and Suzanne. Laura said her mom had left the city for a few days and went to visit Layla in Paris.

"Mom said she doesn't want to know anything about you and feels stupid about what happened on the cruise ship. Her concern is that at this stage of her life and age she acted like a schoolgirl and not the serious woman she had become. What happened on the cruise ship? Why is she so angry with you? She is very upset that she fell for you again and was simply beside herself." He remained silent.

Laura and Jules both called Suzanne and she would only speak to Laura but not to Jules.

Jules then called Suzanne on Laura's phone and when she heard his voice, she told him there was nothing to talk about. "I'm very happy that you and Laura are finally together, the years have not passed in vain."

Jules said, "Suzanne, please forgive me. As we speak, I am in the process of selling my stock and in the process of leaving the business to associates. The only thing I want is to dedicate time to my family." Jules pleaded and asked, "please, please just come back home and we will work this out together. Suzanne, if you are not back by Friday, I will take a plane to Paris to be with you and bring you home."

Suzanne responded that she would return in about two months, she needed time to think and needed time to resolve her situation with him. "It is harder for me now because you are in the picture and spending a lot of time with my daughter."

Jules responded by saying, "Our daughter, Suzanne. Don't act like this, you know what we both felt in the cruise ship. We belong with one another, I have no interest in anyone but you. I think you know that I'm not perfect, Suzanne. Give me a chance to prove to you that my love is sincere. Loving you has always been the best part of my life, don't take this away from me now.

"Suzanne, I need you, I want you. Let me love you, you don't have to love me, I love you enough for the two of us. Let me continue to prove my love to you. I'm a changed man. I'm not the man you met 25 years ago. I am the selfless, humble, loving man you fell in love with in the cruise ship. You felt the same as I did. Don't deny what you felt on the ship. It was real, it was us."

Suzanne was silent, she did not want to discuss their relationship anymore. She was physically, mentally and emotionally exhausted. As though she did not have any energy to continue the conversation with Jules, all she said was, "Jules, I need some time. I will call you when I'm ready to come back home and face you. Enjoy your time with Laura, both of you have years to make up for."

Four days had gone by and Suzanne was feeling she had not healed, but she missed Laura and the excitement of becoming a grandmother and enjoying her daughter's pregnancy. She had been in Greece and now in Paris and was homesick and ready to come back home. She felt like an adolescent running away from home. Layla convinced her to go back home and convinced her to meet with Jules, and if she really felt the relationship had gone sour to just tell him and get it over with.

Suzanne was feeling sick lately and she didn't want to see any doctors in Paris, other than her own. She decided to return home and didn't tell anyone until she arrived at the airport and called Laura to tell her she had arrived. She took a cab to her apartment in the city and when she arrived Laura was there waiting for her.

Hugging her, Laura said, "I'm so happy to see you. I missed you so much and really need you. Please, don't go on any more trips. I've never been without you so long and feel like an orphan."

"I'm so happy to see you too. Laura, you are now five months pregnant and it's starting to show. You look beautiful."

"Mom, my friends are planning a gender reveal party and a baby shower for me in about a month and I want you to accompany me to start looking for a baby store to make a registry and, by the way, don't make plans for Friday. I have a sonogram scheduled and want you to accompany me and receive the sealed envelope with the baby's gender for the surprise on the day of the announcement."

Suzanne asked, "Laura what is a gender reveal party?"

"Mom, it's an event, whether it's your first child or your fourth, where you finally learn whether you're having a boy or a girl. It's a celebration with family and friends and it's called a gender reveal party. That's why I want you to accompany me to give you the sealed envelope. If I keep the envelope I will be tempted to open it up and find out if it's a boy or girl."

"Well that certainly is new! Laura, how will you know if I open up the envelope?"

"Mom, I will know if you open it up. It's a secret, remember. You'll have to open it up or give it to the coordinator and she will fill up a box with baby blue or pink balloons. At the party the box is opened and all the balloons fly out and the gender is revealed."

Suzanne said, "Well, that certainly is new, it definitely did not exist in my times." They both laughed.

On Friday, when Suzanne arrived to meet Laura for the sonogram, Laura said, "Mom, I'm so glad you came, we are a little early. My sonogram is scheduled in about thirty minutes, although they usually run about 15 minutes late."

Suzanne told Laura, "That's fine, I'm in no hurry. When we leave, let's go shopping for you and the baby and select clothes for the baby."

She also told her that she wanted to buy the baby's crib and furnishings.

Laura looked at her mom and said, "Jules-dad has already purchased all of the furniture. He wants Richard, me and the baby to move in with him when the baby is born."

Suzanne became very upset and told Laura, "How could you have planned a move without letting me know, does that mean that I...?"

At that moment Jules walked in with Richard. Suzanne looked at Laura and said, "I hadn't realized that you had invited Jules."

"Mom, I don't want him to miss any important moments. I need the two of you and Richard with me. You are all my family."

Jules and Richard sat next to Laura and Richard looked at Laura and his eyes went back and forth looking at Suzanne and Jules, and he made a funny face. Laura started to laugh and was called by the nurse. They all stood up at once to accompany her and the nurse told them to sit while they get Laura ready for the sonogram.

Suzanne started to read a magazine and speak to Richard, ignoring Jules.

Jules, feeling ignored, asked Suzanne about her stay in Paris and told her he would have picked her up at the airport. Suzanne responded that she had a car waiting for her. Jules then insisted that he would have gone personally to pick her up, with a wicked smile and raised his eyebrows.

Suzanne did not find him funny and looked at him seriously.

They were called in and the doctor started to describe the picture in the screen. When they saw the baby, tears rolled down their cheeks. It was the happiest moment for all of them.

As they were leaving, Laura and Richard got into the elevator and Jules held Suzanne's elbow and let the elevator door close.

Suzanne said, "What do you think you're doing?"

"I just want to talk to you and you won't let me. You don't take my calls, you visit the office after I'm gone and you won't join us for dinner."

"There is nothing to talk about Jules, I'm all talked out."

"Suzanne, you don't believe for one minute that I'm going to let you go, do you? I want to talk about us."

"Jules, there is no us and there will be no us. I spent time in Paris, thinking about you and me and realized that it is difficult to love you. One day you say one thing and the next moment you're back to the same old Jules. For one moment, I thought you were sincere and here we are again, having the same conversation as before. Please don't insist, it's simply over."

Jules argued, "No it's not, I'm not giving up on us." He pulled her to him and kissed her in the mouth and said, "Don't let me go, please."

Suzanne said, "Jules, I'm not ready and I don't think I will ever be, please don't. I don't want to hurt us. I think that for Laura's sake we need to let her enjoy our company and be there for her and the baby. But that doesn't mean that we will be together."

Jules said, "Then there is an us, isn't there? You're just angry with me because I didn't live up to the plans as I had promised."

Suzanne, tears rolling down her eyes, responded, "Jules please, don't make this more difficult than what it is. I want to be alone. It's not about you, it's about me."

Jules asked, "How much more time do you need, I'll wait for you."

"I don't know."

"Suzanne, I know you are angry with me and you have all the reasons to be, but we can rise above this. Come and live with me, I have told Laura and Richard to come and live with us and the baby.

"No Jules. I will not go to live with you."

"Suzanne, we were so happy on the cruise ship, what happened? Are you afraid? I'm afraid too. This is all new to me. I never had a daughter. And now I have a daughter, a son in law, a grandson and you. Suzanne, we are a family."

"Exactly Jules, and whom am I?"

"I don't understand, I love you, I want to be with you. I want to be "us" not just you and me. Why are you making this relationship and our being together so difficult? Is there someone else? Is it the fact that I now know Laura? Is it that you don't feel the same as I do?"

"You're asking too many questions, let's just give the relationship some time. I'm not ready."

"How long Suzanne? Another 20-25 years? When? When will you be ready?"

CHAPTER THIRTEEN

WE'VE ONLY JUST BEGUN

few days later, Suzanne and Laura's friends were planning the gender reveal party. Suzanne and Jules argued because they each wanted the party at their home. Suzanne insisted that it be held in her apartment. After going back and forth they finally agreed to have the baby gender reveal party in a downtown club, because her apartment was too small and they would have the shower party at his home.

Suzanne had hired a party coordinator to decorate the club. She had chosen soft blue and light pink curtains in the background and for the table clothes. She had placed a box in the side of the room which read, "HE or SHE." There were baby cutouts and balloons on the walls and hanging from the ceiling. The decoration was beautifully done. It turned out to be a big gathering.

They had many friends and family members from Richard's side of the family, in addition to their close friends like Mae, Layla and Andrea. Layla flew in from Paris with her husband and daughters.

Most of the guests had already arrived. Suzanne was sitting at the table with Mae, Layla and Andrea. Jules, Laura and Richard stood up and Suzanne said she had an announcement to make. They had moved the box full of balloons to the middle of the room. Suzanne announced she would cut the ribbon to reveal if the colors were blue, for a boy, or pink, for a girl. When she cut the ribbon, dozens of blue balloons started floating in the air. In the balloons it was written, "It's a boy, it's a grandson."

Everyone was celebrating it was a boy. Jules hugged and kissed his daughter, hugged his son in law and grabbed Suzanne and kissed her softly and said, "Thank you for making me the happiest man." They all celebrated as though it were New Year's Eve.

After the party, when most of the guests had left, Suzanne became ill and started throwing up. She had already gone to her doctor's appointments and suspected what was wrong, but did not say a word. Layla and Mae followed Suzanne to the bathroom and they looked at each other and both said at the same time, "Pregnant!" Mae then said that they had disappeared in the cruise ship and said they had the flu. They both started laughing and said they hadn't gotten their vaccine to prevent the flu. Suzanne was not laughing and said that she ate something and, "It must have been the shrimp." They told her to call her doctor and schedule another appointment and laughed. After the party, Mae told Jules he should accompany Suzanne to her apartment because she wasn't feeling well.

Jules insisted on taking Suzanne home and although she wanted to go alone, she was too weak to argue with him. When they arrived, Jules tucked her in and laid down next to her. Suzanne wanted him to leave but he decided to stay and told her he was not going to leave her alone. Jules poured himself a glass of wine and got very close to Suzanne and she started getting very nervous and told him she was tired, it was late and he should be leaving. "Jules, it's late and I really need to wake up early tomorrow morning."

After saying that, she excused herself and ran to the bathroom to throw up again. When she returned she was pale and told Jules she needed to lie down and again insisted that he should leave.

Jules decided to stay because she didn't look well and asked if she wanted to go to the emergency room. She said that she was fine and it was not necessary.

Jules then asked, "Can I at least kiss you goodnight before you go to sleep."

She responded, "Only if you leave me alone, and on the cheek."

Jules then placed his drink on the table, held her face in his hands and as she closed her eyes waiting to be kissed, he kissed her forehead and said, "Good night."

Suzanne got up from her bed, closed her bedroom door to keep him out and after closing the door she put her back against the door and stayed there for a few minutes thinking of him. Jules knocked on the door and as she opened the door, he grabbed her by the waist, pulled her up to him, gave her a passionate kiss, let her go and said, "Sweet dreams."

Suzanne again closed the door to her bedroom and just stood there trying to ignore his presence and her feelings.

Jules started to tell her, "I know you are standing behind the door."

Suzanne asked, "What is it that you want."

Jules responded, "I have pledged my love to you and I know that you love me. You could not have been with me and spent so much time with me if you didn't love me."

She said, "Jules, I don't want anything from you, I just need time," and she went to sleep.

He stayed at her apartment that evening. It was the first time in days that they were together and he wanted an opportunity to talk to her.

The next morning she woke up to the smell of coffee which made her very nauseous, and she ran to the bathroom throwing up again. Jules thought she must have eaten something that afternoon or evening that made her very sick. Jules heard Suzanne moving around in her room and called out her and said, "Have you made a decision about moving in with me?"

She responded that she hadn't given it much thought, although she knew that her daughter was temporarily living there to check the travel time from his home to hers and Richard's work.

"Suzanne, you need to decide before the baby is born in three months, Laura is going to need all the help she can get and you're her mother."

Suzanne had walked to the dining room area where Jules was finishing making a mess with the coffee maker and said, "Jules, I don't think it was a good decision for Laura and Richard to move in with you. It is too far from the city."

As Suzanne spoke, Jules started to get very, very close and smiled at her. "You know, it's frustrating to be around you and not be able to hold your hand or touch your face or whisper something romantic in your ear."

There was a knock on the door and Jules opened the door. It was Laura. Suzanne came out in a robe and when Laura saw them together, Suzanne said, "Laura this is not what you think."

Jules raised his eyebrows and tightened his lips and Laura started laughing. Laura asked if he had slept there and he said, "Yes," and Suzanne shouted from her room and said, "He slept on the couch."

Laura said, "Dad, knowing my mother, you slept on the couch," and smiled.

Jules made breakfast and they all left the apartment together. Suzanne went to the doctor's office to see if the lab results had returned. She had missed her appointment three weeks ago and the symptoms had not gone away. She was very tired and very sleepy lately and couldn't understand why. The doctor told her that they had made a full analysis and that she was fine physically. He asked her several questions regarding the nausea she was feeling, asked if she had gained any weight and she said yes because she had been on a cruise ship and she ate more than usual. He then asked her if her menstrual cycle was regular and when did she have her last period.

She looked at him and knew where he was headed and said, "My daughter is 25 years old!" and he said, "According to your medical file you are 49 years old, and according to your lab reports you're pregnant."

She said, "It can't be, I'm going to be a grandmother in three months," and he said, "And you will give birth in about six months depending on your last menstrual cycle."

Suzanne called Mae and told her to come and pick her up, that she had an emergency. She met with Layla and Mae and, sobbing uncontrollably, she admitted she was not sick. She was pregnant! Mae and Layla laughed and argued about being the godparents. Suzanne told them to stop, they were not acting as her friends. Both said, "Of course we are," and continued laughing. Suzanne said she was more concerned about how Laura would react than Jules. Mae recommended that she first tell Jules and they should both tell Laura.

Laura and Jules were spending a lot of time together at the business, discussing different strategies. Jules was so impressed with his daughter and saw so much of himself in her. He would just look at her and nod, he was so proud of her. Many times they agreed. Sometimes they disagreed, based on Jules's expertise, but she always ended up doing what she wanted. Jules would give her all the flexibility she needed so that she would learn by trial and error.

One afternoon he asked Laura for advice about her mom again. He felt she was still very angry and he didn't know why; after all, he had invited her to move in, told her he loved her and they would be one happy family.

Laura looked at him and said, "You know, dad, for a guy who's been around a lot, married twice, can't you see what mom wants."

"I don't understand Laura, what more does she want."

"She has everything that you can offer her, except one thing."

"What else can I give her?"

"She loves you dad, marry her."

"Marry Suzanne, she won't accept me. I think I asked her already. She will think it's because of you and not her. She has a strange way of thinking. I'm not going to propose now."

"Both of you are so stubborn, I'm surprised that I am not that stubborn. You will have to do something big and surprising for her to accept a marriage proposal at this stage of her life. You need to make the commitment, dad."

"But I thought I proposed to her."

"Dad!"

"I'm listening…"

"I have just the place. There is going to be a benefit concert in the park and I am part of the committee coordinating the event. Each table reserved requires a donation. I will reserve a table under mom's name and invite mom and we will then plan a proposal there."

Suzanne could not believe what the doctor had told her. He had confirmed her fear. She locked herself in her apartment and did not leave it for about two days. The doctor had scheduled a sonogram and Suzanne went with David. She cried the whole time, especially when she was told there were two heartbeats.

Suzanne did not quite understand what she meant by two heartbeats and the nurse smiled and said, "Two heartbeats are two babies."

David was with her and the nurse asked if he was the father and he responded that he was a friend. David took Suzanne back to her apartment and when Mae found out, she called Jules and told him that Suzanne had an emergency and wanted to speak to him.

Jules rushed over to Suzanne's apartment and when he arrived he asked her if she was now ready to move in with him.

She said, "No, Jules, who told you to come by?"

Jules responded that Mae had called him.

Suzanne sat down to tell him that she had decided that she would not move in with him. That she was very happy with the relationship that he and Laura had developed, but she really liked living alone.

Jules said, "That's not acceptable, Suzanne. I want to marry you, I want you to be my wife. And this is not about Laura. I love you Suzanne. I want you to marry me."

Suzanne said, "All my life I have waited for you to ask me to marry you and you never wanted to commit. I don't want you to marry me because of Laura. I wanted you to marry me because you loved me. If you would have asked me to marry you on the cruise ship, I would have said yes, but now it's too late."

"It's not about Laura, it's about you and me."

"Jules, I raised Laura as a single mom, except for the time I was married. I had never been with anyone else except you."

She then said, "Jules I need to show you something."

She picked up a manila envelope on her glass table and showed him the sonogram she had just taken. He looked at the images in the sonogram and asked if they were Laura's, and she said, "No."

"Whose are they? It looks like there're two babies."

"Yes, I know there are two babies."

Jules looked at her and said, "Is this why you were nauseous and throwing up?"

"Yes, and I feel sick!"

"Two babies!"

"Yes."

Jules sat next to Suzanne and put his arm around her and rested her head on his shoulder. They did not say a word for about an hour.

Finally, Jules spoke and told her that he would have never thought that he could be the happiest and luckiest man in the world. He put his hand on her stomach and said, "Thank you God for the greatest blessing."

They remained quiet and he took her to her bedroom and laid her down and laid down beside her and they simply looked at each other holding their hands in front of them and no words were spoken. He kissed her forehead and said, "Thank you, Suzanne."

She had fallen asleep and when she woke she went to the bathroom and Jules was not there. She walked over to the living room and he was standing by the window looking out at the city. Suzanne asked if he was all right and he responded that he couldn't sleep thinking how blessed he was. He said last week when he came over he felt he was the loneliest man with no future or family and even in the midst of all the publicity he was receiving he was very much alone, and today he was a man with a family and it was she who bought him all of this happiness. He would have died last week without anyone to care about him, facing his loneliness and now he was alive and loving every moment of all the wonderful things that had happened. He now knew what it meant to say, "Tomorrow is another day." He thanked Suzanne and said that he would always be with her and that he knew deep down inside that she loved him and was just hurt with his actions and that he couldn't blame her, and asked for forgiveness.

Suzanne looked at him, and how sincere and humble he was, and smiled and said, "We will work it out. My only concern is telling Laura, she has been an only child. She has grown very attached to you, she's pregnant and I don't want her to feel that my being pregnant will in any way make her feel that she is not loved as much by the two of us."

Jules said that both of them would meet with her and tell her the news, they would now do things together and make decisions together.

Suzanne was hesitant, but agreed that they should talk to Laura together. She did not have the courage to face Laura alone. Suzanne was not prepared for her daughter's reaction.

Laura had gone for another sonogram with her husband and when she saw her mother's name on the register did not think anything off it. She simply thought it was another person with the same name because it was not her handwriting. She did not know that David had signed in for her.

That morning Jules wanted to visit her doctor to ask about the special care she needed and what they needed to do. He was so excited he was going to be a father again. This time it was different because he would be there enjoying every step of his children's growth as they start walking, uttering their first words, and celebrating their birthdays. He thought about Laura and he could not have ever imagined how much you could love your children and he felt the greatest love for his grandson and he was now going to have twins. "I never knew so much love and emotion could exist in one's heart."

He said, "Suzanne, I am leaving all of my business affairs. I only want to take care of you, Laura, our grandson and our children. I know you don't want to marry now and I understand why, but let me be next to you and help raise our family together. Let's move to our house in the country, to our home with our family."

Suzanne accepted that she could move at some point, but did not make any promises.

After meeting with the doctor and receiving his assurance that he did not have to worry about the pregnancy, he took Suzanne to her apartment and left to meet with Laura.

That day he and Laura discussed several outstanding business issues. He did not have the courage to tell her anything about Suzanne's pregnancy. That afternoon he sent her two dozen roses with a note saying, "You fill my heart with so much love, Dad."

That afternoon Laura went to visit Suzanne, because she had not gone to the office and to take her the pictures of the gender reveal party. They were both talking about the party and Laura said she and Richard had talked about moving upstate permanently with Jules. She and Richard were enjoying the country life and the traffic was not as bad as they had anticipated. She found a perfect place between two trees for a hammock and one of them was also perfect to hang a swing for her son to play.

She told Suzanne they would keep their city apartment, but once she gave birth they would move in with Jules.

Suzanne was nauseous again and went to the bathroom. Laura asked what the doctor had diagnosed and Suzanne did not respond while she was still in the bathroom. Laura sat in the couch to wait for her and then she saw the large manila envelope with the doctor's letterhead. She thought it was the results of Suzanne's labs and immediately thought there might be something wrong with her mom.

Suzanne walked in and saw Laura with the envelope in her hands and opened her eyes. Laura was looking at the envelope and she asked, "What is this? Do you have something to tell me?"

There was a knock on the door and Suzanne walked over to open the door. It was Jules. As he walked in, he saw Laura holding the envelope of the sonogram and looked at Suzanne and asked her if she had told Laura, and Laura said, "Tell me what? Is there something wrong, are you sick?"

Suzanne answered that she was not sick and before she could say anything else Laura pulled out and read the report and, looking at the images in the sonograms, asked her mom, "When were you going to tell me?"

Suzanne said she didn't know how to tell her and Laura, looking at Jules, said, "Dad?"

Suzanne and Jules were speechless and Jules finally said, "Laura, we didn't know how to tell you. We found out yesterday and we didn't know how you would react. You and I finally met and we have spent some wonderful days together, we are getting to know one another, and step by step building a relationship and I've been giving you and my grandson my unconditional love. I didn't want you to feel that you found me and were losing me."

Suzanne said to Laura, "You are and will always be the center of my universe. I was so afraid to tell you, for fear that you would get angry. I know how much you suffered over not having your father."

Laura said, "Mom, you had sex?"

Suzanne looked at her and said, "Laura!"

"What I mean to say is that you never had any relationship because you worried about me and all of a sudden it's OK. Didn't you think you could get pregnant?"

"No, it just happened, I never expected this at this stage of my life," and she got up and ran to the bathroom again.

"Well, now we really are one big family. I hope you both are happy. When I thought I would now have the two of you, I don't. I am not being selfish, my life is divided again and I'm frustrated right now. I'm going home to my house."

Jules pleaded, "Laura don't leave, I don't think you understand the depth of my love for you. You are my world and nothing is going to change that. You are the daughter of my dreams. I always wanted a daughter and I will never give you up." He walked up to her and put his arms around her and told her, "I love you."

Suzanne had returned and also put her arms around her daughter and said, "I have always loved you. Everything I have done, I have done for you."

Jules told Laura, "Please don't take this away from me, I have been the happiest man alive because I have a daughter who is just like me. I love you, Laura, and our plans can't change. We are now a bigger family. Laura, please tell your mother to marry me."

Suzanne responded, "No, I'm not. I like being a single independent mom?"

Laura left and stayed at her apartment with Richard. She didn't know what to make of the news. When she told Richard, he understood her frustration and said, "Laura as far as I can remember from our college years, Suzanne worked day and night to achieve the success that you both share today. She was always a full time mom. Tired as she looked sometimes, she was always there for you. Now you're married and we are having our first child, don't you think she deserves to share her life with someone? And, after all, he is not a stranger, he's your father."

Laura cried and hugged her husband and said, "Thank you; I really needed that. You've made me realize I did act selfish. I guess I'm just not used to sharing mom."

She then waited a while until her teary eyes had cleared and returned to her mother's apartment with Richard and apologized for her behavior, and both told Suzanne and Jules that they would be happy to share their joy for their pregnancy.

They embraced and continued talking, and when the conversation turned less serious, Laura said, "Well, mom, there is no reason for me to complaint for what has happened. After all, I was the one who told you to take a break and go on that cruise and then told Jules where you were. He followed you and here we are. So, keeping up with my work, will you accept my invitation for dinner tonight? Let's celebrate instead of complaining."

Suzanne responded, "Laura, you have made me so happy today that I'll accept, even if I have to go to the restroom several times in the restaurant."

In the following days Jules continued and tried to convince Suzanne to move to his house in the country. She kept saying no, she was not leaving her apartment and Jules decided to move in and stay with her every night. Jules continued to sleep in the couch and Suzanne finally started feeling better.

Every day, Jules would send a bouquet of flowers to Suzanne and to Laura accompanied with large stuffed animals. He also asked for Laura and Richard to meet him to select the colors for the furniture for the baby's room which he had already purchased. He did not want anybody to buy anything for his grandson. Laura discovered he was such a loving father, just like she had imagined he would be. Suzanne accompanied them to start looking for baby furnishings for the twins. They were all very happy together.

Suzanne kept contemplating the way that Laura and Jules would look at each other and how they discussed their business dealings as though they were old associates. Jules had his hand on top of hers the whole time. They were developing strategic business plans to expand the business in international and Latin American countries. He had all of the experts in place just like she and Laura had discussed.

In the mornings, Jules would cook breakfast for Suzanne and himself and would leave early to finalize his projects and then spend time with Laura. He thought it would be a good idea if Laura moved their office to his office building and they wouldn't have to pay rent. He had just as much office space as she needed, as well as parking space and they would be able to work closer together and he would not have to go back and forth between office buildings.

Laura and Suzanne spoke every day and she told her about Jules's suggestion to move. Suzanne did not want to respond until she was able to see the facilities and the traffic during peak hours.

Three weeks later, on the day of the concert, Laura, Richard and Suzanne showed up with a couple friends of Laura and Richard. There was still one available seat, which Suzanne knew was reserved for Jules, who she supposed was late.

There were several big name bands playing that evening and when a band came on they announced that they were dedicating this song to Suzanne from Jules. Suzanne looked up and had tears in her eyes. She knew Jules was a very special person and she loved him for it. The first song was Joe Cocker's "Sorry seems to be the hardest word," followed by "You are so beautiful to me."

Jules arrived with a flower and asked Suzanne to dance with him. At first she looked around and said no, but everyone at the table convinced her to dance. As they danced they looked into each other's eyes. Their eyes were smiling, their hearts were pounding. He held her hand and her waist as they danced. There were reporters all over taking pictures and there were three big screens showing them dancing. This was their moment, the universe had confabulated to bring them together. As the song ended, Bruno Mars started singing "Marry me," followed by, "Count on me," and Jules knelt before her, pulled out a ring from his pocket, put the ring on her finger, opened his arms and said, "Suzanne, will you marry me?" She looked at him, smiled and said, "Yes!," and whispered, "What took you so long?"

Suzanne had finally decided to forgive and move on. All she had dreamt about had become her reality and it was greater than anything she had ever anticipated. Life was good, it didn't seem as though so many years had passed by. She had deposited all of the past sadness she had experienced in the imaginary bottle she had created in her mind when she did not want to think about something negative. The imaginary bottle had helped her to control her thoughts and emotions, to detach emotionally and move on to the happy place.

After several days, they were at Suzanne's apartment packing. Suzanne came out of the bathroom in a robe and Jules was looking at the big city from the window. They started to walk towards each other, looking at each other passionately and as he slowly began to remove her robe, they were kissing and holding each other ready to give into each other. He was slowly kissing her neck and she was caressing his face and shoulders, when the phone rang.

Suzanne noticed it was a call from her son in law and she said, "Could it be Laura's due?," and as she picked up the phone they looked at each other, exhaled and smiled. When she answered the phone, her son in law said, "We're at the hospital because Laura's water broke and she's going into labor."

They looked at each other and both said, "Grandparents!"

They started laughing, left the apartment, and arrived at the hospital where Laura had already given birth to a beautiful baby boy.

Months after that, today, Jules and Suzanne are looking at a photo album of their wedding on the beach with friends and family, a picture of Mae catching the bridal bouquet, pictures of Laura with dad and mom, Richard and the baby and photos of them in a hammock with their grandson and twin girls. Suzanne has flowers in her hair and they are looking at each other very much in love.

"We've only just begun."